SECRET SAUCE

THE SECRET SERIES

JILL SANDERS

To my sons...

SUMMARY

Trent owns a high-profile restaurant in New York. His food and secret recipes are highly sought after. His personal life mirrors his successful career. Beautiful women hang on his every word. But when his restaurant receives a bad review from a well-known food critic, things take a turn for the worse. When he finally tracks down the food critic, he might just lose more than his secrets to her.

Marina's true identity has been hidden for years. She receives her paychecks in secret and hides in one of the largest cities in the world. But when her secrets are threatened, she'd do anything to protect the person she loves the most.

*T*renton walked into the old building on Fiftieth Street. He'd been looking at the old brick place for a while—staring at it, actually—since it was adjacent to his new loft. He'd had his real estate agent searching for a building all over Manhattan. So far, she'd come up with nothing he liked. Then last week, the tenants of the place next door, an old furniture store, moved out. The place had sat empty since then.

He'd had Jessica, his agent, check on it but the place hadn't come on the market yet. Just a few hours ago, though, he'd watched the owner, a small Korean woman, place a "for rent" sign in the large front window. He'd texted his agent and rushed down the stairs and out the door quickly.

When he'd first approached the owner, he'd been breathing hard and her eyes had gone wide like she thought she was about to be mugged. After he'd caught his breath, he'd grabbed the sign and told her what he wanted.

Now, over a month later, he looked around the building— his building—and thought of all the work that needed to be done. He had building permits locked in his briefcase, along with bids from various reputable construction companies. He also had almost a hundred applicants to interview and train after the kitchens were completed and all his new equipment was delivered and set up. He had the bar staff to hire, stock to order, and tables and tablecloths to order. He didn't skimp on any of the details.

Smiling, he could just imagine how it would look a year from now. Manhattan Nights was going to be his first crown jewel; the doorway that would open up other doorways. He would oversee every part of it himself, adding his touch wherever he could.

CHAPTER 1

ive years later…

MARINA WAS RUNNING LATE. She looked down at the small
paper in her hand and craned her neck in all directions
looking for the right place. She loved her job, but she hated
deadlines. And her shoes. She looked down at the new silver
heels and wondered why she'd bought them in the first place.

As she quickly started walking towards her destination,
she caught her reflection in a store window and remembered
why she'd paid almost a hundred dollars for the pumps. They
made her feet and legs look sexy. Smiling, she picked up her
pace.

Two and a half blocks later, she found the spot. This place
wasn't the style she usually dealt with. It was actually one of
the better-known places she'd gotten a call for. Standing out
front on the sidewalk, she looked up at the beautiful brick
building and the black awnings with simple lettering that
hung over the doors and windows. She wondered why

Reggie, her boss, had wanted her to come to check out this place.

Running a hand down her skirt, she straightened her shoulders and walked towards the large glass doors. When she walked in, cool air hit her face. She took a deep breath and enjoyed it for just a moment. It was another hot summer day, but since she was wearing light clothing, the five-block hike hadn't bothered her too much.

She walked up and gave her name to the maître d'. As he was seating her, she looked around. The wait staff were well dressed in classy black and white. The tablecloths were a nice rich cream. Actually, the entire room was gorgeous. Nothing looked out of place. From the elegant artwork to the beautiful chandeliers, the place screamed class and comfort.

As she sat down, the maître d' handed her a menu and explained the specials for the day. She nodded and ordered the soup, then the maître d' left her to look over her menu. It was her job to know food. Good food. She'd been writing for the Times for over three years now and had, in that time, stepped on a lot of toes. She'd also advanced a lot of restaurants to stardom. Of course, it was all under her pen name. The only two people who knew her real identity were Reggie and Carol down in payroll.

Smiling as the waiter walked over to take her order, she mentally checked off the list of items she would note on. So far, the place was looking to be a great review.

Half an hour later, her food was delivered, and she quickly changed her mind. She ate quickly and left. She frowned the entire way home, wishing she had never stepped foot in Manhattan Nights.

———

TRENT STARED down at his morning paper and started

choking on his coffee. When he recovered, he threw the rest of the paper down and marched out of his loft. Less than five minutes later, he stood in front of his staff and tried not to yell.

"Who is responsible for this?" He shook the paper. It was a quarter past one, so he knew some of his staff would have already read the review.

Angie, his sous chef, quickly looked away, so he knew she'd already seen the piece. Rob, his chef de partie, looked down at his feet. Half of the other staff refused to look him in the eye.

"I want to know who was on staff and what was served, immediately." His voice broke as he tried not to scream.

Steven, his other head chef, rushed out to get him the answers. For the last few months, Trent had left Steven in charge, so he could focus his time on the grand opening of Manhattan Nights' second location, just off of Fifth Avenue.

He stood there and waited for an explanation, thinking that obviously, he'd hired the wrong people to control his kitchen. He'd just have to step back into that role himself again until he could find someone else to take over.

He'd already hired staff for the new location, which was set to open in just under three months. But this review—he looked down at the paper and felt his stomach roll—might set that back.

Steven rushed towards him, his face red, as he held out the schedule. Trent walked into his office and Steven followed him, close on his heels.

"Shut the door," Trent said without looking at the man. As he looked over the list of employees, he noticed that in the last week, Steven's name had been removed three times. "Did you take some time off this week?"

"Yes. I called you and left messages. My sister was sick.

She needed some scans done." Trent knew that Steven's older sister was fighting cancer.

"I didn't get any messages." He looked down at his phone. "You left these on my cell?"

He shook his head no. "I left them on your home line. That's where you said to call."

Trent forwarded his home line to wherever he was so any calls should have been routed directly to him. His frown deepened. The man's answers weren't adding up. "Strange, I never received any messages." He looked over the list. "Can you tell me why M. Jensen, one of the best-known food critics in New York, would claim that our beef tartare was"— he picked up the paper and read word for word— "harder than the bottom of my shoe with less taste than my ex." He tossed the paper down in disgust.

"I'm…I'm not sure. I personally tested everything." Trent stood up and started pacing. "I know this looks bad…" Steven was fumbling with his hands and Trent could see sweat dripping down the man's face. He hated to let him go, especially now, since he'd have little time to find and hire someone else, but a review like this could break his restaurant, especially since it was from M. Jensen.

An hour and one chef later, he walked out of his office with the new schedule in hand. When he pinned it to the board, several staff members walked over and looked at it. He heard some groans, but since he was leaning up against the wall, his arms crossed, glaring at them, everyone just got back to work. Pushing away from the wall, he went and washed his hands and got to work himself. Since he was the only chef until he could find a replacement, he was working every shift until Manhattan Nights' reputation was back up to par.

That evening, they saw a huge drop in guests and over the next few weeks, the numbers continued to drop. It was quite funny how loyal customers who did nothing but praise the food and service before had decided the place was no longer good enough to frequent after reading someone else's review.

By the end of the month, the place was almost empty on weeknights. He had to do something and fast if he was going to keep his businesses afloat. And the first thing he wanted to do was track down M. Jensen and request that the man come in for another review. Or ring his neck.

First thing Monday morning, he marched into the paper and requested a meeting with one of the editors. After hitting a brick wall there, he requested another meeting with a different editor, only to be told that there was a waiting list for reviews from M. Jensen. He left an hour later, more frustrated than before.

When he walked back into the kitchen later that night he noticed that half his staff wasn't in yet. He walked over to Angie while he wrapped his apron around his hips. "Where is everyone?" Angie had been there for him since opening day. She was the first employee he'd hired. In the last five years, he'd never seen her take a day off or heard her complain.

She looked at him and frowned. "Sick." Her blonde hair was tied back in a tight bun at the base of her head. Her blue eyes were always looking around, catching everything that went on. She was almost his height, with a stockier build, but the one thing he admired the most about her was that she knew how to cook. It was something that came naturally to her, not something she had to work at. Her organization skills were the only thing stopping Trent from moving her up. When he'd first hired her, they'd had a brief personal relationship that had become a solid working friendship.

Wiping the sweat from his brow, he realized he'd worked harder this month then he had when he'd first opened the place. Not only had he been running the kitchen and staff, he was also interviewing chefs for Steven's replacement whenever he could. So far, he had three chefs that he liked. All three would come in for a full-day interview that included them running the kitchen and staff for a complete meal.

At closing time, he walked back to his loft, totally exhausted. He still had a pile of papers to go through for the new restaurant and would no doubt be up-all-night playing catch up.

When he walked in, his machine was flashing with new messages. Listening to them as he grabbed a beer, he heard his longtime friends talking about baseball season starting and groaned.

It wasn't that he didn't like baseball season—he loved it. Unfortunately, the season started in three weeks, which meant that he'd need time free for practices and games, something he couldn't afford yet.

At least not until he'd hired a new chef, set M. Jensen straight, and earned back his reputation and customers.

arina was running late again, but this time it really mattered. She jogged a little faster, the running shoes she'd put on before leaving her apartment cushioning her steps.

She turned the corner just as the last bell rang and smiled. Slowing down to catch her breath, she waved to Miss Keith, Tommy's second-grade teacher. There was a small line of kids standing next to her dressed in little tan pants with dark blue shirts, all neatly tucked in and clean.

Tommy, her pride, and joy, stood next to his teacher, waving at her. She smiled and felt her world settle as she walked towards them.

"Hi," she said, a little out of breath.

Miss Keith smiled. "Good afternoon. We were just wondering what happened to you. Usually, you're already here."

"I'm sorry. They were fixing our water heater. How was school?" She bent down and looked into Tommy's hazel eyes, which almost matched hers perfectly.

"Great! We got to hold a butterfly today."

"You did?" She added excitement to her voice as she hugged his little body. It was the best feeling in the world when his little arms came up and hugged back. She knew that one day he wouldn't be so enthusiastic about receiving her hugs or about talking to her about his day, so she was determined to enjoy every minute of it. "Are you ready to head out?"

He nodded, and she noticed that he was due for another haircut as his dark hair fell over his eyes.

"Bye, Miss Keith."

"Bye, Tommy. See you on Monday."

As they walked the half-dozen blocks towards their small apartment, hand in hand, Tommy talked about everything that had happened to him in the hours since she'd dropped him off.

When they reached the stone-steps leading up to their building, they stopped to talk to Mr. Johnson, one of their neighbors. He was out walking Rascal, his seven-year-old boxer.

Marina had lived in the building less than a year, but already knew, and more important, trusted everyone in the six-apartment building. She could afford something nicer and bigger, but circumstances called for safety now instead of comfort.

When they walked through their door, Tommy tossed his bag down and raced towards his room, throwing his shoes and tie. She chuckled and walked behind him, cleaning it up. It was almost a daily occurrence. She tried to convince him that being neat was cool, but he was seven.

When she walked into his room to hang his clothes, he was already dressed in his play clothes and collecting his bag of cars.

"Can I go play with Mark and Juan?" he asked, giving her one of his famous pleading looks.

She smiled. "Yes but promise you will be back in one hour." She tapped his watch and smiled when he looked down at it and studied the numbers for a while.

"Five after five." He looked up for her approval. When she nodded, he bolted towards the door then stopped, put down his bag of toys, rushed back to her, and hugged her tightly. "Thanks, Mari." He turned and was gone, leaving her sitting on the floor, smiling after him.

She heard him slam the front door and run next door to Mark and Juan's place. The two boys would no doubt be waiting for their friend, who had a standing playdate with them every day. Julie, their mother, was a close friend. Whenever Marina was on assignment, she trusted Julie to pick up Tommy and watch him until she could make it home. They even sometimes took turns picking up the three boys.

She walked down the hall to the desk area between the small kitchen and the even smaller dining room. When she flipped up her laptop, she saw several new emails from Reggie.

She knew that her line of work could cause ripples in the restaurant business. She'd been working as a critic long enough to know which places would have issues with her criticism.

Manhattan Nights was one of those places, and the email from Reggie only confirmed her fears. This one was going to be messy.

She'd stopped questioning her opinions years ago. When she'd started this job almost seven years ago, she had tried to point out the positives in every place. But even after those reviews, she had received threatening letters and emails. Some of the business owners had even shown up at her home, trying to convince her to change her opinion. She had quickly started writing under a pen name to protect herself. Reggie was also very good at keeping them away.

Sighing, she emailed him back that she would give Manhattan Nights another try. Pulling up her calendar, she placed it on her schedule for next week. She loved her job, really. It was something she was not only good at but enjoyed.

She wrote three different columns, all using different pen names. Her favorite was the food critic column she wrote as M. Jensen, not only because she could write off her meals, but because it allowed her to try new things.

She also wrote a self-help/home improvement column as Mary Contrary. She loved organizing and sharing new and improved ways of saving space or teaching others how to clean up spills or handle those out of town guests that just won't leave.

Her least favorite article to write was the relationship help desk. Readers wrote in and asked her opinion on relationships. Since it had been over a year since she'd been in one, she found it harder and harder to write as Meddling Marci. When she'd started writing the article, she'd been in a relationship for seven and a half months. She'd thought she knew it all back then.

Looking up from her computer, she frowned at her reflection. She found it easier to get her work done with the large mirror hanging over her computer. Every time her eyes wandered off the screen, they would zero in on her own face, and her eyes always told her to get back to work. It was a love/hate relationship she had with herself.

Now, however, she wasn't working; she let herself remember the last date she'd been on. It wasn't Steven's fault for breaking off the relationship, not really.

When her sister, Caterina, had shown up on her doorstep one night begging for help with little Tommy fast asleep in her arms, how could she have turned her away?

Of course, Steven hadn't taken the news well that she

would be playing full-time mom for a while. But his breaking it off had made it easier for her to move and step out of the limelight, which had been harder to do than she'd thought.

She leaned her head back and thought about how her life had changed in such a short time and wondered if she would ever feel free to date again if there was someone out there that could understand her circumstances and look beyond them.

***

TRENT WAS THINKING about killing someone, and he knew just who he was going to start with: M. Jensen. That man was getting on his nerves. Not only had he been getting the runaround from the paper, but now he'd found out that the man had actually made a second pass at his place a few days ago. This review hadn't gone in the papers. No, it had come directly to him in the form of a letter explaining what was wrong with his restaurant and staff.

By the time he was finished reading it, he wondered if the man had been in the right restaurant. He took a few seconds to calm down before stepping out of his home office and walking across the street to Manhattan Nights. He'd printed the email and unknowingly crinkled it in his hands as he walked.

Dear Mr. Walker,

I understand that my last review was a hard pill to swallow; however, I pride myself on my opinions. Since you requested I come in for a second pass at your restaurant, Manhattan Nights, I thought it best to contact you directly instead of publishing this review.

I revisited your restaurant and am sorry to say my original opinion still stands. Although your building is lovely and your wait staff very courteous, your food is still lacking.

I've included a brief list of items I found unsatisfactory below.

The Seared Scallops were rubbery and lacked any true flavor. Your Whole Roasted Organic Chicken, a meal I was assured was one of your specialties, was not only served burnt but had what seemed to be a full jar of pepper on top. The dessert, the Plum and Almond Sweet Tart was hard and chewy like it was weeks old.

When I revisit a restaurant, I usually see some improvements since my initial visit; however, I would have to say that Manhattan Nights has not only not improved but has gotten worse. My suggestion is for you to get out into your own dining rooms and try the food your staff is serving customers. If you find it satisfactory, get out even further and visit some of the best restaurants this great city has to offer. Compare what they have versus what you are serving. Maybe then you will see how Manhattan Nights is lacking.

I hope you understand when I decline any further requests to visit your establishment in the near future, at least until I'm assured that you've made the necessary changes to make my dining experience what it should be and not just a waste of my time.

Sincerely,

M. Jensen

Trent crinkled the paper even more as he walked quickly through the dining room back towards the kitchen. His new chef, Trey, stood behind the chopping block, a large knife in his hands, quickly chopping some carrots. The man was a few years older than Trent was but had only been a chef for three years. The man was a genius with spices. Since hiring him, they had added several new dishes to the menu and the dining rooms were filling up again.

Angie was busy at her station but stopped and looked up when he walked by her. "What's up, boss?" She walked over to him, wiping her hands on a towel.

"Gather the troops, would you?" He walked past her into the small office and waited until there was a knock on the door. Then he walked out to once again try and get to the bottom of what had happened, why it appeared that someone was sabotaging him by making sure M. Jensen was served some of the worst food to go out of his kitchen.

As he talked, he watched everyone's faces. Some looked ashamed, others looked scared. He couldn't see guilt on anyone's face.

The only possibility was that there was a leak somewhere. Someone standing before him knew M. Jensen. Knew what the man looked like in order to serve him bad food. In the last few weeks, Trent had taken to personally spot-checking the food that left his kitchen. He'd even gotten in the habit of walking around talking to his customers and asking how their meals were. Everyone had been completely satisfied. Their plates had been empty, and they assured him they would return.

He just couldn't explain how M. Jensen had gotten two bad meals unless it was sabotage.

After informing his staff that Trey or Angie would now check every dish that left the kitchen and be personally accountable for its quality, he walked back across the street. When he sat down at his computer, he decided it was high time he started playing detective.

Punching a few keys on his laptop, he started his search into M. Jensen. There had to be something out there on the man.

Two hours later, he wanted to pull his hair out. Short of a few fuzzy pictures from restaurant security cameras, no one had a clue who the man was. Some had even speculated that he was a she, which was starting to make sense, especially since the fuzzy pictures all appeared to be of the same woman. There were five photographs in all. He couldn't really tell if it was the same woman, only that she had medium-length dark hair with short bangs, pale skin, and long sexy legs. At least from what he could see in the photos.

He clicked on the paper's website and started reading through some of her back articles. After wasting another hour there, he picked up the phone and called an old buddy.

Carter Edwards was an old college friend, but it wasn't Carter he was after. Carter knew Ethan Knight, ex-special forces agent, and owner of Knight Enterprises, a search-and-protect type of business. The man made millions from either protecting high-powered clients or tracking down hard to find people.

"Hello?"

"Hi, Eve, Trent here. Is Carter around?" He'd also gone to school with Eve, who was now happily married to Carter and expecting their first child in the next few weeks.

"Oh, hi, Trent. Sure, let me get him." The phone went silent, and then Carter answered.

"How's it going down there in New York?"

"Good. You guys are sure missing all the excitement by living clear up in the sticks." He smiled, remembering their large home on the bay in Maine.

"Oh, there's still plenty of it around here. Just yesterday, Eve had me paint the baby's room. Pink."

Trent laughed. "A girl, huh? Congratulations."

"Thanks. What's going on in your neck of the woods?"

Trent told him what had been happening and less than fifteen minutes later, he hung up and dialed Ethan Knight's number.

A woman answered, and he remembered that Ethan was married to Ann Rhodes, the journalist who had broken the story about the plot to kill her father, the Texas senator.

"Hi, Ann, this is Trent Walker."

"Hi, Trent, how are things on the East Coast?"

"Doing great. Is your husband there, by chance?"

"Sure." He heard her giggle. "But he'll have to wrestle our twins to make it to the phone. Give him a minute."

"That's okay." He could hear a burst of giggling. "Maybe you can help me answer a question. If someone worked for your paper and wrote under a pseudonym, would there be any way for someone like me to find out their identity?"

"Oh, that's a tough one. If the paper is committed to keeping their employee's identity safe, probably not. Not even accounting will provide you with their real name."

"Hmm, that's what I thought."

"Here's Ethan. Maybe he can help you."

"Hey, Trent, what's up?"

An hour later, Trent got back to work on his laptop, knowing that the best man for the job was now on the case. Ethan would contact him if he could track anything down about the elusive M. Jensen.

The next time he looked up, it was a quarter to six in the morning. He'd done everything Ethan had suggested to find out more about the man, all with the same results as before. It was almost as if the man had been born three years ago. He knew that M. Jensen was most likely not the man's real name, but so far, he had been unable to find out who would have paid off the very notable and seemingly reliable reviewer to trash his place.

From what he could tell, his only potential enemy was the owner of the restaurant across the street from where he was planning to open the second Manhattan Nights. He'd spent almost two hours researching the man and his family. Jake Baird had owned Cairo's Bistro for almost ten years. Prior to that, the man's father and grandfather had owned the small bistro.

When Trent had picked the location to open his second restaurant, he'd given little to no thought about the small place across the street. Especially since he didn't believe they would be in direct competition.

The bistro was very small and had a much lower profile

than Manhattan Nights. Cario's served quick breakfasts, easy-on-the-pocketbook lunches, and pizzas and calzones for dinner. Nothing like his place at all.

After spending most of his night confirming his initial thoughts, he was assured that Jake and Cario's were not behind the attack. Answering that question only filled him with more.

Standing up from his leather desk chair, he stretched and decided a run might help clear his head. He jogged up to his stairs and switched into some sweats and his old Princeton T-shirt.

He headed out the front door with questions buzzing around his brain. As he started his run, he thought about everything he'd learned so far. He'd spent the entire night scanning the internet, but he kept coming back to those five pictures of the brunette. Something in his gut told him that the woman knew something. After all, the five restaurants that had published those photos of her had been visited and critiqued by M. Jensen the same day the pictures were taken. He knew it was more than possible that the same woman had visited five restaurants in New York. He had visited hundreds of different places in just the last year, himself.

What were the chances that the same woman would be photographed on the very day that the reclusive reviewer happened to visit? It was just too coincidental.

He was just hitting the halfway point in his morning jog when he spotted her. He was so shocked that for a moment he forgot the smooth motions of running and almost tripped over his feet. Then, he thought he was going mad from the lack of sleep and blinked a few times. When the woman continued to walk towards him, he stopped dead in his tracks and stared right at her.

It had to be her, he told himself. The dark shoulder-length hair, the short spray of spiky bangs. Those legs. He watched as she stopped, looked right at him, and blinked a few times. Then she opened the door to one of his favorite coffee shops and walked in without a second glance in his direction.

Now what? he asked himself as his feet carried him towards the door.

CHAPTER 3

*M*arina sat down at her favorite table and when John, one of the waiters, came and took her order, she ordered her usual breakfast roll and coffee. Then she pulled out her laptop and got to work.

When the chime above the door rang, she glanced up and saw Sexy Runner. Or so she had been calling him since she'd first seen him over a year ago. She must have passed the man on the street at least a dozen times a month since first spotting him a block from her new place. Never once had he spared her a glance, until today.

It had caused her heart to skip and then beat so fast she'd fumbled and almost dropped her computer case. Now she watched him walk into the coffee shop and stand at the counter. She'd seen him in here a few times as well and even remembered that he always ordered a large, cold green tea.

Now, he stood up at the counter and looked up at the menu like it was written in a different language.

She watched as the clerk, a very young college student who always got her order wrong, flirted with him while taking his order. He paid and then walked over to wait for his tea.

She was shocked when he glanced towards her and smiled. She blushed and quickly looked back down at her computer screen, which she realized she'd yet to turn on. Feeling like a fool, she quickly powered up her laptop and tried to look busy.

Men like that didn't notice women like her, she told herself. No, he probably had a string of skinny blondes lined up and waiting their turn to have a date with him. She could just imagine it now—he would laugh and grab two women, pulling them close. He would—

"Is this seat taken?" a deep voice asked above her. She glanced up quickly, only to discover that her computer glasses caused everything to blur farther than two feet. Quickly pulling them off her nose, she tried not to let her chin drop when she realized that Sexy Runner stood next to her table, waiting for her reply.

"Um," she tried to think of an excuse. *Why?* her mind screamed at her. Let him sit down. Let him come home with you. Let him...

"Good." He smiled and sat across from her. "Whew, it's getting hot out there." He took a large drink of his cold tea. "I didn't interrupt your work, did I?" He leaned a little to glance at her computer, which she realized she hadn't even logged in yet.

"No, I was just..." She flipped down the screen and tucked her hands under the table to hide the shaking. Being this close to him caused her entire body to quake with needs that had lain dormant in her for so long.

"I've seen you around, haven't I?" He looked at her again. His eyes ran over her face, her shoulders, and then crossed down to look at her legs, which were crossed and poking out from under the small table.

She was just thankful she'd worn her new Jil Sander skirt and blouse and her favorite green heels, which matched the outfit perfectly. The fact that they made her legs look longer and thinner hadn't escaped her attention. And by the heat in his eyes, it hadn't escaped his either.

"I come in here often," she said as smoothly as she could. "I think I've seen you around here, as well."

He smiled. "That must be it." He reached his hand across the table. "Stephan Trenton Walker the third, at your service. But everyone calls me Trent."

"Marina." She reached out and felt the warmth as he took her smaller hand in his.

"Marina, what?" he gently asked as he kept hold of her hand, causing the warmth to spread up her arm and shoulder.

"Just Marina. Mari," she said, not able to blink when she looked into his sky-blue eyes. She hadn't known what color they were before today. He'd always run with sunglasses on or had been too far away for her to tell. Now, she wished he was wearing shades. The pale blueness of them caused her to want to stare into them forever.

"Mari." He smiled again, showing off white teeth that had the slightest slant to them, which caused him to look sexier and a little dangerous, especially with the stubble on his face, which was dark and longer than she'd seen on him before. She was sure he had always shaved before jogging before, but this time he looked like he'd been up all night and had forgotten.

His dark hair was slicked back and held the slightest curl. She'd seen it when it was shorter and a little longer, but he'd always maintained the same style.

"Well, Mari, I do hope you don't think me too forward, but I was hoping you would join me for dinner sometime," he said smoothly, convincing her that he was well practiced at asking strange women out.

Something in her mind screamed at her to decline, but her mouth hadn't received the memo, and before she knew what she was doing, she'd agreed.

"Wonderful." He smiled and released her hand finally. Instantly, she missed the warmth. "How about I pick you up this Friday around seven?"

This time her mind won before her mouth could agree and give out all her secrets. "How about I meet you somewhere?"

He looked at her as if trying to gauge her, and then he smiled. "Sounds great. Name the place."

She thought about it and quickly blurted out the last restaurant she'd given five stars to. It was only two blocks away and was a perfect place for a first date.

"See you then." As he stood, he handed her a napkin with his name and number scribbled on it. She must be losing it; she hadn't even seen him write it down. "Give me a call if you change your mind." He leaned closer to her and spoke softly, his husky voice going deeper. "I'm sure I can change it back."

She closed her eyes and an image flashed into her mind so quickly, she blushed. Looking up, she smiled slightly and nodded. "I'll be there."

"Good. See you Friday, Marina," he said, just before he walked out the door.

Mari watched the clerk behind the desk sigh as Trent jogged away from the building, heading back in the direction he'd come.

She must have sat there for a few minutes, looking out the window, before John walked over and set her blackberry scone and vanilla iced coffee in front of her.

Shaking her head, she nibbled on her scone as she wrote

her weekly articles and answered a handful of emails from her mailbox.

She always enjoyed working in the corner booth here. People rushed around her and outside the large glass windows. She typed away until all her work was done, then glanced down at her watch and realized it was around lunchtime. She was due to visit a new restaurant today and was excited to try the new Thai place.

She paid and left a good tip for John, then decided to walk the three blocks to the restaurant. She hadn't made it to the gym in over a week and was feeling a little guilty about the two scones she'd eaten.

As she walked along the busy streets, she was conscious of her surroundings, as she'd learned to be over a year ago, always paying attention to people around her, looking for faces she knew and wanted to avoid. She'd once had to duck into a physic shop to avoid a run-in with one of her old neighbors.

Since the day her sister had disappeared, she'd been on high alert. So when she turned one of the last corners towards the restaurant and felt a familiar zing on the back of her neck, she quickened her pace and ducked into an old candle shop. Spending a few minutes pretending to look at the wonderfully scented candles was hardly chore. A few minutes later, she stepped closer to the window to look out and see if she could spot the cause of the sensation. When the busy streets looked clear of her lingering past, she quickly bought a small vanilla candle and made her way to the Thai restaurant.

She really did enjoy her work. A lot of people assumed that critics just got paid to eat food, but there was so much more to her job than just eating. She had to assess every aspect of a restaurant. She made her usual rounds to the restroom, usually trying to peek inside the kitchens, but that had caused her problems, so she left most of that information out of her reviews. Her trained eyes took in every part of the front dining area and the staff, down to the details of how the tables were set. When the food was delivered, she tasted everything. If she enjoyed it, she ate the whole thing. If not, she simply set it aside after critically thinking about what was displeasing.

She ate in relative silence. If anyone were to look at her, they would think that she was a young woman who was lost in her own thoughts.

This time she lucked out and, after finishing the entire plate, sat back and thought about a dessert she'd add to complete the wonderful meal. The job was heaven, except when it wasn't. She didn't like giving negative criticism, but it came with the paycheck.

New York was one of the top restaurant cities in the world, and as an owner of a restaurant in one of the largest cities, you had to make sure you conformed to certain guidelines. She always looked at it as if she was doing them a great service in letting them know the areas they could improve upon.

After having some of the best baked-coconut rice pudding she'd ever had, she walked back towards her apartment to write up her review. Pleased with the whole ordeal, she didn't see the man who followed her half a block away.

TRENT WALKED into his apartment sweaty and feeling a little more confident that he'd found the person responsible for causing his business to lose steam for the past two months. Now all he had to figure out was why.

After showering, he walked into his office and shot out an email to Ethan. Then he began a search of Marina Jensen.

After almost thirty minutes, he realized he had hit another brick wall.

Maybe her last name wasn't Jensen? He widened his search, adding in the paper's name. Still nothing. Oh, she was good, he thought as he shut down his laptop and looked at the clock. It was close to dinnertime, and he realized he'd only had a quick roll and some tea that day. Grabbing his jacket, he sprinted towards Manhattan Nights through the heavy rain that had started to fall.

After talking to a few of his staff, he headed into the dining room and was shocked to see how few people were there. There were a few upcoming parties they were hosting this weekend in the larger private dining rooms, but they needed regular customers on weeknights to keep the place running.

Grabbing a table, he ordered and looked around, wondering what was wrong. He doubted that one bad review could have caused all the customers to disappear.

He ate his meal in silence and critiqued every bite as he watched every wait staff member and every customer that walked through the door. When he was done with the meal, he thought about Marina and those damn sexy legs. Her dark coffee eyes held so many secrets. She'd said she'd seen him around, but he couldn't ever remember seeing her. He doubted he'd pass up a woman who looked like her, at least not without talking to her, flirting with her, getting her number. It wasn't as if he was going around picking up every good-looking woman in Manhattan, but if he'd seen her on several occasions, he would have noticed.

Maybe she knew exactly who he was? Maybe that was the whole point? Since opening the restaurant, he'd had his fair share of women stalking him. The first year he'd been in business, he'd thrived on the extra attention he'd gotten from women. It seemed like he'd had a new one on his arm every weekend. Being a celebrity restaurant owner had its perks. The second year he'd been in business, he had slowed it down and had only dated a handful of women. In the last three years, he'd seen only four. His longest relationship had lasted only two months. It wasn't as if he was getting burned out on women; he was just seeing the same pattern over and over and had started looking for something new. An image of Marina flashed in his mind.

She was unlike any woman he'd dated in the past. For some reason, he'd always migrated towards tall, slender, and very blonde women. They had always been easy on the eyes and hot in bed, but nothing much to hold a conversation with.

He wondered if Marina would be any different. One thing was sure—the woman had secrets. He was even more determined now to find out as much about her as he could. Even if it meant sleeping with the enemy. That thought caused him to smile. Friday couldn't come soon enough.

The week seemed to take forever to pass. There had been several things to distract him, such as approving the final touches on the Manhattan Nights II plans and hiring and firing a few staff members. It seemed that some of his staff found it amusing to post nude photos of themselves taken at their work online. It had been after hours, but that fact hadn't let them escape his wrath. Teenagers. He'd sworn he'd never hire anyone under twenty again but knew that wasn't possible since most of his busboys and cleaning crews were under twenty. Had he ever been that cocky? He laughed when he remembered some of the wild parties he, Mitch, and Carter had gone to in college.

When Friday morning came, he filled his time trying to find out more about Marina. He was beginning to wonder if she'd given him her real first name. Ethan had yet to contact him, other than a short email telling him he'd look into the new information he'd provided.

When he dressed for the evening, he thought of all the ways he could get more information from her. Since he thought she knew exactly who he was, he'd have to do it smoothly.

If she really did know he was the owner of Manhattan Nights, then she would know exactly why he had asked her to dinner. He had to play his next move very carefully. First things first—he had to find out if she knew who he was. Then he would be able to move onto finding out why she was trying to ruin him and Manhattan Nights.

CHAPTER 4

Marina was nervous. She'd changed outfits at least a half-dozen times. Julie sat on her bed, watching her patiently and giving her opinion on each outfit. Finally, Marina settled on her classic beige dress. The material twisted around her, giving off the appearance that she had more upstairs than she did. She finished off the outfit with some of her favorite jewelry and her sexy open-toed, high-heeled sandals.

Looking at herself in the full-length mirror, she smiled. She'd taken the time to curl her normally straight hair. Her bangs accented her eyes, as did her makeup. She dabbled on some of the expensive French perfume her sister had sent her from her trip to Paris a few years back. Then dashed on her deep rose lipstick as she stood at the front door mirror.

"I really appreciate you letting Tommy spend the night," she said to Julie.

"Don't worry about it." Her friend smile at her. "They'll be crashed out in front of the TV before I know it. You just have a fun time."

Just then, Tommy, Mark, and Juan came running in. Both of Julie's boys looked like her, however, Juan had the darker skin, hair, and eyes of Julie's ex-husband, where Mark had light blond hair like Julie's high school sweetheart.

"Mom, can we *goooo* already? We want to show Tommy our new games," Mark said, looking impatient.

Julie rolled her eyes and crossed her arms over her chest. "In just a few minutes." Then she looked over at Marina. "Go, have a great night."

Marina hugged her, then knelt down to Tommy and hugged him. "You be good for Julie. Don't ask for sugary snacks and make sure to brush your teeth."

"I know, I know." He pushed her away from a little when she held onto him too long. "I'll be good."

She kissed him on the cheek, leaving a little smear of pink that she wiped away with her thumb. "Night."

Grabbing her silk purse, she dashed for the door, trying hard not to look back. This was the first night in a year that she'd be apart from him. She'd had Mark and Juan over to spend the night before but hadn't let Tommy spend the night down the hall once in the past year. It wasn't that she didn't trust Julie; she didn't trust herself to be away from him for that long. Her sister had entrusted her to watch over him until she could return, and she took that job very seriously.

As she walked the two blocks towards Via Dante's, she took several deep breaths to try and calm herself down. She'd been on plenty of dates, but they seemed like ages ago. She'd dated Steven for almost a year prior to getting Tommy.

What should she talk about? She started wondering if she was going crazy. This is just a date, she tried telling herself over and over. Then she remembered who it was with. Hot runner, Trenton Walker. She knew nothing about the man except that he jogged almost every day and looked damn sexy doing it. She'd been almost infatuated with the man since the first time she'd seen him over a year ago. He'd been her fantasy man, and now she was going on a date with him.

Stopping at the front doors of the restaurant, she took a moment to straighten her skirt and make sure her hair and lipstick were still in place using the reflection of the glass doors.

"You look beautiful," a deep voice said behind her.

She gasped a little and spun around. He looked even sexier in dress clothes. She'd never seen him dressed up since he'd always been out running and had been wearing sweats or shorts.

"Thank you." She couldn't help but smile back. "You look great in clothes," she blurted out, realizing too late what she'd said.

He chuckled and took her hand. "Thank you,"

"I mean real clothes." She blushed even more.

His smile grew more as he nodded. "Shall we?" He pulled open the heavy doors.

She nodded and thought that maybe she shouldn't speak for the rest of the night, to avoid embarrassing herself even more.

They were seated at one of the tables near a large gas fireplace. The intricate stonework reached up two floors. There were balcony tables that looked down on the main floor. The low lights and the candlelight around the room made everything look dreamy.

"Do you come here often?" he asked, looking around.

She shrugged her shoulders. "I've been here a few times. I absolutely loved their Soupe à L'oignon last time I was here." She smiled as she read over her menu.

When she looked up, he had a sparkle in his eyes and she realized he'd been watching her very closely.

"Have you ever eaten here?" she asked.

He shook his head. "I've been sticking close to home. Although I've been told I need to get out more." He smiled at her and she felt like she was missing the joke.

"So, what do you do for a living?" She set her menu down and tucked her fingers together under the table. When she felt nervous, she tended to fidget, and this was the best method of keeping it at bay.

He tilted his head. "I'm in the service business. How about you?"

She'd thought about this. It wasn't as if she liked going around lying to everyone but giving a vague description of her work had been the best course.

"I'm a writer." She smiled and picked up her menu again.

"Really?" He sounded interested. "Books?"

She chuckled. "No, although I've always wanted to." She set her menu down again. "Service? As in waiter or something else?"

His smile faltered for a moment, and then he nodded. They were interrupted by the waiter as he took their orders, and when he left, Trent steered the conversation in a different direction. The rest of the night, the conversation flowed smoothly. She'd tried to get more information about him, but the more she tried, the more he wanted to know about her, so she'd backed off and allowed him to lead the conversation.

By the time dessert was delivered, she'd found out that he lived alone in an apartment he'd renovated a few years back, he played baseball with some of his buddies from Princeton, where he had attended, he was born and raised on the East Coast, and he had a sister Rachelle, who was ten years younger than him.

She still didn't know exactly what he did for a living but judging by his clothes and the fact that he'd attended Princeton, she doubted that he was a waiter as she'd been led to believe.

BY THE END of the date, Trent was growing frustrated. The woman knew how to sidestep a question. She was also toying with him about knowing who he was and what he did. Did she think he was buying it?

He sat across from her in the low light of the room. Most of the dining guests had left, causing the room to feel more intimate. Her hair and eyes sparkled in the firelight. He couldn't explain it, but every time he saw her chest rise and fall, he wanted to hold his breath in anticipation. Which got him thinking that it had been too long since he'd been with a woman. Not that Marina wasn't attractive. Hell, he couldn't remember seeing anyone sexier than she looked sitting across him now.

If he was going to get to the bottom of why she was trying to ruin him, he had to keep his wits about him, or so he kept telling himself.

He needed to play his cards very carefully.

One thing was for sure—by the end of the evening, he knew he had to see her again. She'd built up a hard shell on the outside and it would take more than one dinner to crack it.

He was telling her a story from his college days to keep her from asking more questions. She laughed, and the rich sound sent waves of desire spreading throughout his entire body.

How could a laugh do that to him? Damn, he thought when she looked down at the silver watch around her thin wrist.

He looked at his and was shocked at the time. Looking

around the room, he realized that only a few other people sat in the dim room. "I'm sorry. I didn't realize I'd kept you so long." He stood and walked over to pull out her chair for her.

"Oh, it's no problem." She stood and smiled at him. "I've really enjoyed our time."

"Me too." He took her hand as they walked towards the doors. "I'd like to see you again."

She looked over at him and smiled, then nodded. "I'd like that."

He quickly calculated. "I'm pretty busy this weekend." Then he had an idea. "Do you like watching baseball?"

She chuckled. "I've never seen a live game, only on TV."

"Really?" He smiled and held open the door for her. "Perfect."

When the cool evening air hit them, he saw her shiver.

"You've forgotten a coat." He tsked at her as he took off his dinner jacket and wrapped it around her shoulders.

"I guess I was too anxious about dinner to think ahead," she whispered as she looked up at him.

He couldn't help but smile. The sweet scent of her perfume hit him, causing his libido to jump. He pulled her closer on the dark sidewalk and let his hands linger on her shoulders. Her hair was in loose curls around her face, and her short spiky bangs accented her dark eyes. Then he glanced down at those lips again. They'd been begging for his attention all night with their strawberry coloring, their fullness. He'd wondered all night if they tasted as good as they looked. Before he knew what he was doing, he'd dipped his head to find out.

When his lips touched hers, he forgot all about who she was, about why he was there. His only thought was to take more. To somehow enjoy every centimeter of the soft lips under his.

Her hands came up as her fingers pushed through his hair, pulling him closer as he angled his lips over hers. When he used his tongue to taste the sweetness of her lips, she met his move, and he felt a strong flash of desire as they tasted and played with each other.

He ran his hand over her hair; its silky softness called to be touched. Running his hand below the heavy curls, he cupped her neck and felt her shiver again. Her body was pressed up against his and he felt her breasts press against his chest. He had to have more, he told himself.

Pulling back a little, he looked into her eyes. "Come back to my place."

Her eyes were closed, but when he spoke, they cracked open. He could see the desire in the dark crystals. Then she shook her head and blinked.

"I can't. Not yet." She looked up at him and he could see fear there.

He sighed and for a moment his mind cleared, then screamed at him. *What are you doing?*

He nodded, not trusting his mouth to relay what it needed to. He wanted to pull her closer, to peel that sexy, tight dress off her curvy body, but instead, he stepped back and took hold of her hand. "At least you can let me walk you home."

Her smile faltered. "I'll take a cab."

He nodded as they stepped to the curb. "If you want, we have a game tomorrow in the north fields at Central Park at one."

She nodded. "I'd love to watch."

He couldn't help but smile. "Great. I'll see you then." He waved a taxi over. As she got in, he leaned down and placed another kiss on those sweet lips. "Goodnight, Marina."

"Goodnight." She smiled back.

He stood there and watched as the cab drove down the street and took a left two blocks down.

So much had happened in the last few minutes that he needed the cool air to clear his mind. It was almost six blocks to his place and now he'd be walking without his dinner jacket since she'd forgotten to give it back to him. He didn't mind. He had a closet full of the things.

His mind kept flashing back to that kiss. It had been a long time since he'd kissed someone and felt what he'd felt with Marina. Actually, he realized it had been a long time since he'd kissed anyone. He calculated it and realized that the whole review fiasco had put a huge damper on his love life. Four whole months had gone by without him going on a single date.

Disgusted at himself, he smiled when he remembered how wonderful she'd felt in his arms. How her lips had felt and tasted under his... Even now, as the cold seeped into his every pore, he could feel the warmth of her breasts pushing against his chest.

As he quickened his pace, he thought about what he'd learned over dinner. It had been difficult, at first, but halfway through the meal, after he'd started talking about his college days and family, she'd opened up a little bit more about herself.

She had an older sister, Trina. She hadn't mentioned where she was or what she did, just her name. She had talked about their childhood growing up in Philadelphia, where her parents still lived in the house she'd grown up in. She had moved to New York right after high school and had attended night school while working as a writer. She hadn't mentioned where she worked, which caused him to believe he was really sitting across from the bane of his life over the past few months.

But his biggest clue had come earlier on in the evening

when she'd talked about loving the Soupe à L'oignon at Via Dante's. He was dying to get back to his place and his computer to check old articles and see if there had been a critique on that particular dish.

If so, he would know without a doubt that he'd just dined with the elusive M. Jensen herself.

CHAPTER 5

There were times when Marina's wished she could speed up time. Early that next morning was one of them. When she'd gotten home, it had taken her hours to finally settle down. She could have used the short walk in the cool air to help calm her body down, but since she didn't want Trent to know where she lived, she had jumped in a cab and taken the short ride home.

She'd taken a long bath and had even done some yoga before finally flipping on the television and falling asleep to an old episode of *Friends*. She was woken around two in the morning by a phone call. When she reached over and answered it, there was only breathing on the other end. Hanging up, she sighed and wished that there was a way to make all crank callers pay.

The next morning, she was woken when Tommy came bouncing in. He was jumping up and down on the bed before she realized she'd promised Trent she'd watch his game today. Not once had she thought about Tommy. She didn't want to take him; she didn't know Trent well enough to spring her entire situation on him, yet.

Her mind cleared as Tommy grabbed her face with his little hands and asked.

"Is that okay? Can I go with them?"

"What?" She sat up a little and hugged his little body. He always felt warm and sticky at the same time and she loved the mix.

He sighed and rolled his eyes. "Mark and Juan are *going to the zoo today.*" He emphasized the words like she was slow. "They wanted me to go with them. Can I?" He pulled out of her arms and started jumping on his knees on her bed. "Can I?" he repeated until she laughed and grabbed him up again.

"Yes, yes," she said over and over. "But only if you give me a kiss." She tickled him until he almost hyperventilated.

"Yeah!" He started to push out of her arms, but then came back and gave her a sloppy kiss.

"Mmm, maple syrup. Did Julie make pancakes?"

He giggled and nodded. "They're waiting for me." He tugged out of her arms again.

"Well, then you shouldn't keep them waiting." She moved to get up and smiled when she realized he was no longer in the room. As she walked down the hall, she heard him banging around his room for something. Peeking her head in, she asked,

"What are you looking for?"

"My bin-oc-u-lars." He pronounced it carefully and she smiled when it took him two times to say it correctly.

"Why do you need your binoculars?"

He sighed and looked at her as he placed his hands on his hips. "To see the animals of course. You can't go on a saphar-rtid without them."

"Safari," she corrected.

"Safari," he said, trying the word out. "It's like my jungle show. Can I wear my green floppy hat?" he asked, rushing around the room.

She quickly helped him find both his hat and his binoculars and gave him his green backpack with a few snacks and a bottle of water in it.

"There, now you look like you're going on a real African safari," she said, tugging down his hat.

"Thanks, Mari." He hugged her and rushed towards the door. "See you later."

She smiled and waved as he rushed out. A few minutes later, Julie texted her.

- How was the date?

- Wonderful. I'll tell all later. Thanks for taking Tommy with you today.

- No problem. The boys will love it. We should be back around six. Since I know they will want pizza and ice cream after.

- Thanks again

She dressed and cleaned up the mess they had made in Tommy's room, then looked at the clock and realized she had two more hours before Trent's game.

Usually, Saturdays were full of Tommy. They would either go to the park or shops or, if it was cold out, they would spend the day playing games. It had been a long time since she'd had a whole day to herself. She didn't quite know what to do with herself now.

It was funny how in just over a year, her entire life had changed. She sat at her little makeshift desk and opened her laptop.

The image of her sister and Tommy popped up on the screen. She wished she knew where Trina was, but it had been her plan to completely hide until she knew that it was safe to come back for her son.

Sighing, she decided not to think about her sister and instead focus on last night. Trent was so different than she'd imagined he'd be. She hadn't realized how much her mind had come up with in the year she'd spent daydreaming about him.

He was a perfect gentleman. He was funny, sexy, and smart. How could she ever have imagined all that? Then something he'd said last night flashed in her mind. He'd wondered if she wrote books.

She'd wanted to write a book ever since a college professor had suggested she use her writing skills for something more entertaining.

Opening a new document, she stared at the screen until something came to her. She spent the next hour punching away at the keys. When she wrote for the paper, she thought of it as work, but now, glancing down at the few pages she'd written, she realized she was actually having fun.

The next hour she spent fussing over her hair and make-up as well as picking out the right outfit. She finally decided on a pair of her designer jeans with a crimson blouse over a black silk tank top. She'd purchased most of her clothing in her previous life, as she called life before Tommy. She could remember spending most of her paychecks on clothes, shoes, and accessories. She had a closet full of items that she hadn't worn since she'd chosen her solitary life.

She glanced at her reflection in the hall mirror as she walked out her front door. She was thankful she'd picked her flats to wear when she arrived at the park and had to walk through a grassy field to get to the small stands that sat along the ball field.

She was anxiously looking around for Trent among all the people when she felt a familiar zing up her spine. Turning around, she smiled when she saw him walking towards her. Her breath hitched, and her heart jumped when she noticed what he was wearing. His gray uniform stretched tight over every inch of his muscular form. She'd seen him in loose sweats and dress clothes, but nothing had prepared her for seeing every curve in the light material.

He smiled when he noticed her eyes slowly running over him. She couldn't help it, her face started to flush and heat. All of a sudden, she wished she'd worn something cooler instead of the long-sleeved blouse and jeans.

"Hi, you're just in time." He nodded towards the field to his left. "We're over here. You can sit with Mike's wife, Terry." He motioned towards a young blonde woman sitting in the small bleachers. "They were married last year. Terry is a school teacher at St. Martin's Grade school." He waved at her as they got closer. "Mike's a fireman." He nodded towards a huge muscular man who was currently stretching his arms over his head with the rest of Trent's teammates.

"How do you know all these men?" she asked, looking around nervously.

He chuckled. "Some from college, some from work." He nodded to Mike. "Some have saved my butt on various occasions."

"You'll have to explain that one to me later."

He laughed. "If I know Terry, I won't have to. She'll tell you all about it during the game," he said as they walked up to where Terry sat, smiling.

After introductions, he jogged towards the field, leaving her alone with the blonde.

"So, how did you two meet?" Terry asked right away.

"Well, actually, I've seen Trent around for the last year. He's been jogging in my neighborhood and up until last week, he'd been running right by me." She shrugged her shoulders. "Then last Monday he walked into my favorite coffee shop and asked me out."

Terry laughed. "That man is smooth." She shook her head. "He's never brought someone to a game before. He must have really enjoyed the date."

Marina laughed. "I'd like to think so." She turned a little and looked at Terry. "Now, what's this about your husband saving Trent?"

Terry laughed. "Not literally. Mike's a fireman, but it had nothing to do with a fire." Terry looked off towards the field as the game started. "You see, Trent was on a blind date, and Mike just happened to be at the same restaurant on one as well. When they met in the bathroom, they came up with a plan to ditch both women, since things weren't going so well." She chuckled. "After that, they became each other's blockers. You know," she continued when Marina just looked at her questioningly, "the person who calls or shows up in the middle of a blind date to end the evening."

Marina laughed. "I guess I've never had cause to have a blocker before."

"Neither have I. But back then, Trent and Mike had friends that were always trying to set them up."

"How did you meet Mike? If you don't mind me asking."

"Not at all." They stopped and cheered when Mike hit the ball and ran towards first base. When he'd made it to the base, they sat back down. "My friend Jenny set us up on a blind date." She giggled. "Needless to say, Trent was called off when he called halfway through dinner."

Marina smiled. "Does Mike still play blocker for Trent?"

Terry shook her head. "Not for a while. His friends that always used to set him up are now both happily married men living in Maine somewhere."

Marina smiled and waved as Trent walked up to bat. "How long have they been playing?" she asked, not taking her eyes from Trent's backside.

"Almost three years now. Mike and I were married last spring and I haven't missed a game yet. It's kind of addictive." They both stood as Trent hit the ball and raced towards first base.

They chatted the rest of the game, stopping to cheer when the game called for it. By halfway through the game, Marina was enjoying every minute of the game. The game finished a little over an hour later with Trent's team in the lead.

When he came up to the stands, he was covered in sweat from his last home run. "Usually everyone likes to get together at Harry's Pizza Parlor afterward for beers and a pie."

"Sounds good." She tried not to sound too excited.

"If you want, you can come back to my place while I shower and change."

She nodded and felt a zing of excitement at being able to see his place.

"So how did you like the game?" He nodded when Terry went down to meet Mike.

"I'm loving it. It a lot better than watching it on television." She smiled.

"So, what have you been up to today?" he asked as they started to walk towards the line of people.

She smiled. "I started writing a book."

"Really?" he asked, his eyebrows going up as he looked at her.

She nodded. "Your idea." Then she laughed, "Well, sort of. I guess you can say you put the idea in my head."

"What's it about? Don't tell me it's one of the lovey-dovey kind." He frowned a little and she noticed a small crease between his eyebrows.

She laughed. "No, it's a self-help book about organizing your life." His eyebrows shot up again.

"That's wonderful. I think." He smiled at her.

She felt the need to explain further. "A year ago, I moved from a twelve-hundred-square-foot apartment into one barely six hundred square feet. I've always been an organized person but moving into such a small space really caused me to rethink my skills. Now, after a year, I think I've done pretty well." She laughed. "Julie, my neighbor, and friend is always amazed at how Tommy and I fit into what she calls a shoebox apartment."

He was silent for a moment. "Tommy?" His question threw her for a loop. She'd been so excited about telling him about the book that she'd let the most important word slip from her lips. Tommy.

"My nephew." She turned and was thankful that a few of his friends had stopped right in front of them and started chatting about the game and where they were all heading for a pie and beer.

When they finally left the field and started heading towards his place, she noticed how close it was to her own apartment and frowned a little when she realized it was right across the street from Manhattan Nights. Since he was busy unlocking the gate to let them in, she doubted he'd noticed and decided to keep it to herself. After all, just because she'd had a bad experience at the restaurant didn't mean everyone had.

When the gate opened, she was shocked to see a large private garden area that sat between two tall buildings. As they took the outside stone steps up to two large wood and glass doors, she tried not to feel nervous. She hadn't even known places like this existed in the city. Not only was the brick building beautiful, it was huge. And from the looks of it, he was the only tenant upstairs. There were three little shops that sat on the ground floor outside of the privately gated area.

"Is this all yours?" she asked, nodding towards the garden below.

"Yes, part of the perks of living in an older area." He

smiled as he opened the door. "I'll just be a few minutes." He motioned for her to follow him inside.

When she stepped in, she held her breath. The place was not only huge but beautiful. The older architecture had been salvaged during a recent remodeling. All of the classic wood beams had been saved and gleamed with newness. Even the hardwood floors looked authentic.

"It's lovely," she said as she looked around.

"Help yourself to anything in the fridge. I'll be quick." He headed up a large iron and wood staircase as she walked around the large main floor.

The furnishings were simple and masculine yet had a slight touch that was unmistakably feminine. Most likely from a decorator, she decided. The huge windows opened up the room, letting in enough light that she doubted he ever needed to turn on the classic hanging glass bulbs, except at night.

The living room and kitchen were separated by a large stone bar area. There was a small dining table and chairs off towards the windows on the other side of two huge wood beams. Expensive artwork hung on the walls, and rugs that no doubt cost more than an entire year's salary for her sat on his floors.

The more she looked around, the more she felt like she was way out of her league. What was it he said he did for a living? Service? What kind of service? So many questions started popping into her head that the only way to calm herself down was to start listing off things she did know about him.

He'd been raised in New York. He had a younger sister. He'd gone to Princeton.

There her mind stopped. Princeton. Why hadn't she seen it before? The answer was so clear now. His family had money.

Instantly, she was on guard. Brandon, Tommy's father, was from a wealthy family. If there was one thing she had learned about the rich, it's that they always stuck together in matters of family and had enough power to cause problems if they wanted to.

Her mind was telling her to run, but her feet were glued to the wood flooring. She heard the shower cut off and wished more than anything that she knew more about him. Then she noticed a stack of paperwork by his phone and decided that a little look wouldn't hurt; after all, it was lying on the counter for anyone to see. Rushing over as quietly as she could, she started looking through the unopened mail.

The only thing she could tell was that he used the same power and television service as she did. He hadn't lied about his name, or that this was indeed his place. Every letter was addressed to him at this location.

She set his mail back down and walked to the glass windows and thought about her next step.

CHAPTER 6

When Trent walked downstairs, fresh from a quick shower, he saw Marina looking out the glass windows at Manhattan Nights. He decided to try and get something, anything from her.

"Nice place." He nodded towards his restaurant when he stepped up next to her.

"Hmm?" She turned to look at him. When he nodded again, her eyes followed his direction.

"Oh, sure. I guess. I've only eaten there a few times. Are you ready?" she asked, looking a little nervous. When she'd walked into his place, she'd looked excited and curious. Now, however, it looked like she was jumping out of her skin and eager to get out of his apartment.

"Sure." He reached for her hand and pulled her close. "Just one thing first." He pulled her into his arms and kissed those sweet lips again.

All throughout the game, his eyes and his thoughts had kept wandering back to those lips. He'd kept telling himself that he had built up last night's kiss into something it hadn't been. When he tasted her again, he realized he'd been wrong. She tasted as sweet as he remembered, even a little sweeter.

At first, her body was tense, but when he started running his hands up and down her back, he felt her relax in his arms.

"I thought I had imagined it," he said as he pulled back a little and looked down into her eyes.

"What?" she asked quietly.

"You," he said before dipping his head and claiming those sexy lips again. When he heard her moan, he pulled her closer until he could feel her chest rise and fall with her breath. When he finally pulled away, he couldn't help but smile at the lost look in her eyes. He was doubly pleased to know that she no longer felt uncomfortable.

"What do you say about getting some pizza and beer?"

"I…" She looked around like she was trying to come up with an excuse.

"Oh no, you don't," he said lightly. "No backing out now. Besides, the ladies will kill me if you don't show up. Who else is going to talk to them while us men sit around and brag about our big win?"

She smiled a little and nodded. "Let me just text someone first." She pulled out her cell phone from her pocket and walked over to the window.

"There," she said a few seconds later, "all set."

They walked a few blocks to Harry's, a place he frequented almost as much as his own place. Harry, who had been dead since the early seventies, had been replaced by his son, Carson, and Carson's children, Bryan and Rose. When they walked through the door, Bryan smiled and waved at them, calling out, "They're in the back." He nodded and continued on with a large pie on his shoulder and plates in his hand.

When they walked into the back, everyone called out and

cheered. They shook Trent's hand and punched him on the shoulder. He kissed all the women on the cheek.

By the time they settled down, he had a beer in his hand and a slice of pie in front of him the size of his face. Smiling, he looked over at Marina and watched as she used her knife and fork to cut little pieces out of the large flat pizza slice.

He chuckled and leaned close to her. "You're going to have to pick it up and get those pretty hands greasy."

She frowned a little and then set the utensils down. "I was hoping to avoid it, but I think you're right." When she bit into the pizza, a slow smile formed on her lips. "Oh, this brings me back." She nibbled on the next bite.

"Oh?" he asked as he took a large bite of his slice then washed it down with some of the coldest beer in the city.

She nodded her head. "Our folks would take me and Trina to Mr. Magoo's Pizza parlor for our birthdays. We would eat pizza and play games until we were sick."

He smiled. "When did you stop spending birthdays at Mr. Magoo's?"

She smiled over at him. "I think it was Trina's seventeenth birthday."

He laughed and took another sip of his beer. Even the greasy pie and cold beer couldn't get the desire to taste her again out of his mind.

He knew he was walking on dangerous ground. After all, he needed to find out what her game was and if someone was pulling her strings and why. But he just couldn't get her out of his mind.

He knew it was true that you had to keep your friends close and your enemies closer. But everything in his mind screamed that she wasn't either of those things. She was something else, something he'd yet to discover. One thing was for sure—until he did, he was going to play it very safe around her.

As they left the pizza place, he again tried to walk her home. She was quick to jump into a cab and leave again, but not before she promised to meet him on Thursday for coffee at the coffee shop where they had met.

He walked back to his place and opened his computer. The morning had been too busy to do any research, so he spent the next hour or so reading through past reviews of M. Jensen's.

There were two reviews in the past four years for Via Dante's place. One of them for Soupe à L'oignon and one for their Poulet Basquaise. Both of them rave reviews.

Then he looked for any reviews for the little coffee shop, A Latte Fun. There weren't any, nor were there any for any pizza joints or burger shops. It seemed that M. Jensen had expensive tastes.

Then he remembered that she'd said she lived in a very small apartment with her nephew, Tommy, and wondered where her sister had gone. Maybe she'd died? He wished she'd given him her last name. He knew not everyone had their private lives available online, but over the course of the next hour, he searched the name Trina, Tommy, and Marina and went through every article that mentioned one or all three names.

When the sun came up, he didn't feel like he had gained any more information. Heading up to grab a few hours of sleep, he set his alarm to wake him just after the lunch rush.

He was just a few hours into his sleep when his phone started shrilling on his nightstand. When he looked at the time, he cursed and wondered why his phone was going off. Then it started ringing again and his head cleared.

"Hello?" he barked into the phone.

"Hey, um, is this a bad time?" Ethan asked.

"No," he said, sitting up and rubbing his hands over his face to try and wake himself a little more. "What's up?"

"Well, I think I've found something."

"Hang on a second, will you? I want to go down to my computer."

"Sounds good. I've forwarded everything I've found to your email."

"Great, hang on." He set his phone down and stood up, then cursed when he realized he'd walked out of the room without the phone. Grabbing it up, he quickly made his way downstairs. "Okay, what's up?" he asked, opening his email.

"As far as I can tell, M. Jensen is a woman by the name of—"

"Marina Jenkins," he read in Ethan's email. It was her. He looked at the attachment and saw several grainy pictures of her entering restaurants.

"Yeah, the kicker of it is, her sister is Caterina Jenkins." Trent's mind was still foggy, and he couldn't place the name. "You know, the woman who had an affair with US Congressmen Brandon Hughes."

Now he remembered. The woman had claimed to have had a child by the congressmen. His mind finally caught up with him. She'd talked about her sister Trina and her nephew Tommy, whom she was now living with.

"Thanks, Ethan." He felt a knot in his stomach.

"Sure thing. I hate to disappoint you, but I couldn't find any reasons for why she would try to burn you. As far as I can tell, she's never been on the take. She lives in a hole of a place, pays her rent and taxes on time, and doesn't even own a car. If she's on the take, she's hiding her money pretty well."

"Hmm, maybe it's something else." He thought about it.

"What? Like blackmail?" Ethan asked.

"Sure, why not. If she's babysitting her sister's kid…"

"I checked into that idea myself. It was another dead end. As far as I can tell, every dime she earns is accounted for."

"Maybe it's not money they are blackmailing her for."

After hanging up with Ethan, he spent the next hour going over Ethan's proof and searching Marina on the internet. He found several pictures and newspaper articles about her sister, Trina. He even found a grainy photo of the sisters together.

When he finally made it upstairs to shower, he felt exhausted and had a headache coming on. He knew he was due to work the kitchen that night and wished more than anything that he'd hired two new chefs instead of just one. He only had to fill in two nights a week, but with his extra job of playing detective, the hours were killing him.

As he crossed the street, he thought of all he'd learned in the last few hours and wondered what he was going to do with the knowledge. He had to be careful about taking his next steps with her. Should he call her? Confront her? Or should he keep playing along with her game of pretending she didn't know exactly who he was? Maybe she didn't?

Walking in the back door of the restaurant, he was so preoccupied with thoughts of Marina, he almost ran right into Angie.

"Sorry." She grabbed hold of his arms, so she wouldn't topple over. "I guess I wasn't looking where I was going." She chuckled a little.

When he'd first hired her, Angie had been driven and focused, like someone had lit a fire under her and there was no stopping her from going in the direction she'd chosen. However, less than two years later, she'd lost her focus and had started acting more like a drone. She was still one of his best assets, but the lack of spark had caused him to pass over her when choosing a head chef.

In the five years, he'd been open, he'd had seven head chefs besides himself. Out of all of them, three had been women and they'd been some of his best employees. He'd had high hopes for Angie and seeing her fall short was almost like a personal jab.

"No problem. How was lunch shift?"

She shrugged her shoulders. "Not bad. Not the best, but not bad." She sighed. "Are you on tonight?"

He nodded. "Oh, I was just going to grab a slice of pizza and a cold one. I thought you'd like to join me," she said.

A slice and beer sounded wonderful. He frowned. "Can't." He leaned against the door frame. "Until things start picking up around here, I'm stuck covering when I can."

She nodded. "How about tomorrow?"

He sighed as an image of Marina popped into his head. "Between here and the new place, I'm keeping pretty busy… Maybe some other time?"

She nodded and then continued to walk out the back door. He turned the corner into the kitchen just as a loud crash sounded as someone dropped a whole stack of plates. He groaned out loud, knowing that it was going to be a very long night.

———

"What do you mean, you quit?" She could hear the stress in Reggie's voice.

"I didn't say I was quitting, I said that I would quit if you didn't give me some time off this next week." She stood her ground. After all, she knew how to handle getting time off from her boss. Reggie was the kind of man who was all bark, especially when it came to her.

She could hear him sigh into the phone, but she also heard his back molars grind as he thought about it.

"Why does it have to be this week?" he asked.

"I've told you. Tommy's school is going to Boston for a field trip and I'd like to go with them."

"Fine, but I expect you to have this week's articles in my email before you leave."

She started to say thank you, but he interrupted.

"And I expect the following week's the day you get back."

She frowned a little. If she had to write up next week's articles as well as this week's, that would mean that she would have to drag her ancient laptop with her and find some time to work in the hotel while helping chaperone a dozen kids under the age of eight. But she'd been through worse.

"Deal."

When she hung up a few minutes later, she smiled as she dialed Miss Keith's cell number to let her know that she could make the trip.

She was very excited about the trip. She hadn't been to Boston for almost eight years.

After talking to Miss Keith, who had insisted she call her Rebecca, she walked into Tommy's room and told him the good news. He jumped up and down on his bed.

"I think this calls for ice cream," he said as his eyes grew. He had a handful of weapons in his arsenal, and sad eyes were the A bomb of them all.

"Maybe," she started, and then held up her hand to stop him from begging. "But after dinner."

He let out a quick whoop and jumped off the bed.

"Can we have pizza?" he asked as he hugged her leg.

"Noooo," she laughed. "Not if you want ice cream afterward. You might even have to eat Brussels sprouts and spinach." She grabbed him when he groaned, and then she started tickling him.

He giggled and screamed, "Yuck, I hate Brussels sprouts," at the top of his lungs.

When she picked him up, she noticed how much bigger

he was than the first time she'd held him. The kid was growing up too fast, and Trina was missing a lot of it.

She always grew sad when she thought of her sister not being there for her son, so she quickly tickled his belly, which made him giggle, causing all her sadness to disappear.

After their pizza and ice cream, Tommy fell asleep in her lap as they watched his nightly half an hour of television.

Carrying him to his room, she decided she would wake him up a few minutes early in the morning, so he could shower; he was too tired for his bath this evening.

Just as she walked into her living room, her phone rang. When she answered, there was heavy breathing again. This was the fifth call this week, and she was just about to hang it up when she heard a low voice. "Stay away from him."

She shivered then hung up the phone quickly and decided to change her number first thing in the morning.

When she'd just settled back down in front of the set to watch the news, her cell phone rang. Her heart skipped a few beats until she saw Trent's name on the screen. Taking a few breaths, she answered.

"Hello?"

"Hi." Just hearing his voice made her breathing hitch. "I'm not interrupting you, am I?"

"No." She smiled and sank back into the couch, trying not to imagine him in his sweat-shorts with no shirt on, sweaty and sexy as sin.

"Good. I was hoping I would catch you. I only have a few minutes, but I was hoping that you'd like to do dinner again this Friday."

She frowned. "I can't." She listened for the awkward silence.

"Got a hot date?" he joked, winning points from her.

"No, I'd have a hot date Friday if I was saying 'yes.'" She smiled when she heard him chuckle. "I'm chaperoning my nephew's field trip to Boston. We leave in two days and won't be back until Tuesday."

"Wow, you are gutsier than I thought."

She chuckled.

"Can I see you before you go?"

Her smile fell away, and the familiar flutter was back in her stomach. "I'd like that."

"What are you doing now?"

"Watching the news."

"If you tell me where you live, I can be there in two minutes." His voice grew soft.

"I…" She didn't know what to say. Could she trust someone with her secrets? Her mind was screaming that he knew too much already, that she should keep this one more detail from him. At least for now. "How about coffee tomorrow morning?"

"That can work." He sounded more lighthearted. "So your work just lets you take off like that?"

"My boss was understanding." She smiled and tucked her feet under her.

"So, I was thinking you should bring the kid to our next game."

"He'd like that. When's your next game?"

"Saturday, but since you'll be out of town, you'll miss that one. We have one the following Thursday night."

"We'll see," she said, biting her lip.

"I have to go." She heard a phone ring. "I'll see you in the morning."

After hanging up, she couldn't stop smiling. She thought she wouldn't be able to fall asleep, but when she finally made it to her room, she drifted off as soon as her head hit the pillow.

She dreamed about Trent kissing her in a grassy field. His lips felt warm over hers as his hands traveled over her shoulders. As in many of her dreams, she blinked and was whisked away to another place where they lay in the warm sun along the soft white sand. Their clothes disappeared as his hands traveled over her skin. He kissed her until she felt like she was spinning. He looked down at her and said her name, but instead of his sexy deep voice, she heard Tommy's soft little voice repeat her name over and over.

Opening her eyes, she looked up just in time to see Tommy lean over her and puke all over her comforter.

"Oh, baby." She pushed the soaked blanket away and carried him to the bathroom just in time for him to get sick again, this time in the toilet.

When she felt his forehead, she discovered that he had a slight fever. Pulling off his soaked pajamas, she ran a warm bath for him. Deciding they could both use some cleaning, she sat down in the tub with him and held him as he moaned with discomfort. When she finally pulled them out of the cool water, she poured a little Children's Tylenol for him. He sat on the couch as she changed her sheets and threw the soiled ones in the wash.

When she walked back into the living room, he was fast asleep. She carried him to her bed and snuggled down next to him and tried to fall asleep through the worry.

By morning, she knew that he was in no condition to go to school. She texted Trent that she would have to cancel, and no sooner had she hit send, her phone rang in her hands.

"What's wrong?" He sounded concerned.

"Nothing, Tommy's just got a touch of the flu. I want to stick close to him this morning." She smiled over at the small bundle wrapped up on the couch, watching cartoons.

"Let me come over. I know a great chicken soup recipe that cures all."

She felt bad for canceling and had really looked forward

to seeing Trent before leaving for Boston, but she just didn't know if she could trust him.

"No, really. Thank you, anyway. I think we'll just curl up and watch cartoons. Thank you for the thought, though."

She listened to the silence for a while. "Okay, but if you need anything let me know."

She sighed with relief. "I will."

After getting Tommy to nibble on some dry toast, she settled down with him to watch the cartoon channel. When he fell asleep in her arms just around noon, she carried him back to his bed and decided she'd try to get some work done.

Flipping open her laptop, she glanced at the mirror above her desk and was thankful she had declined having Trent over. There were dark circles under her eyes, and her dark hair was in tangles. Even her short spiky bangs stood up on one side. She was a mess. It would have taken at least an hour to make herself look presentable, and she didn't want to spare that time with Tommy.

How had the kid become the most important thing in her life? She'd hardly seen him the first six years of his life. Her sister had lived just north of Boston in a small one-bedroom apartment. She'd hidden her pregnancy from everyone, including her only sister. After Marina had moved to New York, she and Trina had just gone separate ways. Marina had strived to make something of herself, to prove to her family that she was worthy. Trina, on the other hand, had taken a turn towards the wild. She'd spent most of her nights partying in Boston's clubs, drinking and probably doing drugs. When Trina had showed up a year before she finally left Tommy with her, Marina had been shocked to find out that she had a nephew at all, let alone a five-year-old one. Even their parents hadn't known they were grandparents. It had shocked them all. Less than a year later, right after Tommy's sixth birthday, Marina had opened the newspaper and was shocked to discover a picture of her sister with a US Congressmen.

Things had taken a turn for the worse after that. Trina had shown up on her doorstep hysterical in the middle of the night. Tommy had been asleep in his mother's arms.

Trina had walked around Marina's apartment rambling about how Brandon was threatening to take Tommy away from her. Apparently, the congressman's current wife wanted her to have a paternity test on Tommy. If the test was negative, they were threatening to sue her for spreading rumors that he was the father. If the test was positive, they threatened to take him away from her, claiming that she was an unfit mother.

First thing in the morning, Marina had called her lawyer. The conversation had left her feeling discouraged. Money could apparently buy you anything and the Hughes family had enough money to get what they wanted, or at least enough to make her sister suffer for the rest of her life if she decided to fight against them.

A month later, Marina had woken up to find a note on her countertop from her sister. Trina had devised a plan and had outlined it in a four-page letter.

Marina would watch Tommy for one year while Trina laid low. After all, Brandon Hughes wouldn't come looking for Tommy with Marina since she worked for the paper and had connections.

It wasn't a safe plan or even a smart one and, at first, Marina thought about calling social services. But within three days of being with the little boy, her heart had melted. After seeing a photographer following her and Tommy at the grocery store, Marina had packed up her belongings and moved into her current apartment under a different name.

Her new landlord had assumed she was running from an ex and had taken the cash deposit and rent with few questions in the last year. No one living near her knew the whole story; at least she didn't think they had guessed it.

Tommy called her Mari and no one seemed to question why. She thought that maybe he was too young to really remember his mother, so she made sure to talk about her often.

Looking down, she realized she'd been zoning long enough for her computer to fall asleep again. Punching a few buttons, she logged into her email and started scrolling through her inbox.

She stopped at one titled, "I know where you are." Her fingers shook as she clicked it open.

I know where you are and what you're doing. You can't keep him. He's mine. I will do everything in my power to stop you.

She felt light-headed and stood up to pace. How had the Hugheses found her and Tommy? Sitting back down, she checked the email address and did a little research. The email address was apparently a temporary account.

There wasn't a signature or even a hint that it was Brandon Hughes or anyone who worked for him. She'd run into the man several times before Trina had finally gone into hiding. He'd threatened to sue Marina as well, but back then she'd had little invested in her sister's situation and in the little boy who would steal her heart. Now, just the thought of losing Tommy made her palms sweat.

A million thoughts went through her mind. Had Brandon found her through her job? No, Reggie had promised to keep her secret, and she'd known and trusted him for years. Then how had he found them? An image of Trent flashed into her mind. Could he have something to do with this? It was interesting that Trent had shown interest in her one day out of the blue. But she had seen him running for almost a year. It couldn't be him.

Then who? How? Maybe he had hired a private investigator? After all, she wasn't an expert at covering her tracks. The paper had her social security number. The school had a copy of Tommy's information. They had assured her they wouldn't share it with anyone, but still…One couldn't hide forever.

For the rest of the day, she worried about what she should do next while she nursed Tommy back to health. By nightfall, she'd worked herself into such a state, she felt a fever coming on.

CHAPTER 7

Trent sat on the bench outside of Marina's apartment and wondered if he should just go up there and knock on the door. When she'd called to cancel their morning meeting, he'd wondered what her game was. He'd gone for his morning jog and had ended up outside the address Ethan had given him.

It was an old stone building that looked like it had seen better days. He knew she was on the second floor but didn't know which windows hers were.

He found a bench across the way and sat down to watch and see if she'd come out. He was far enough away that he could easily duck down an alley before she'd see him. After he'd been sitting for a while, he realized that the same black sedan had gone around the block a dozen or more times. The windows were tinted, and he could only make out enough to tell that it was the same person driving it. He continued to watch as the sedan passed up parking spot after parking spot. It was going slower than all the other cars and had even stopped once in front of Marina's building.

He pulled out his cell phone and snapped a picture of the

car and plates just out of curiosity. Maybe Ethan could look into who owned the car. Could this be her contact? Could this be the person paying or blackmailing her to destroy his business?

Ethan had given him some homework for the next time they talked. Trent had to come up with a list of people who might want to destroy Manhattan Nights. So far, the list was short; he only had four names written down, none of whom he could imagine would go this far to destroy him or Manhattan Nights.

When the sun started to go down and he hadn't seen Marina leave her building or seen the sedan in a while, he got up and jogged back to his place. He wanted to text her to make sure everything was all right with Tommy but didn't want to feel like a stalker. Even though he had just spent the better part of his day watching her building.

As he jogged the outside steps, he thought about the last time he'd been with her. He didn't understand what was so appealing about her, but he knew he had the desire to be with her again. He enjoyed the way she felt in his arms, how her lips felt under his. The way she smiled and laughed made his heart skip.

After showering, he was happy to hear his phone chime with a text message.

-Sorry about today. Tommy's feeling better. Can we try for tomorrow morning?

-Sounds good. I missed seeing you today.

It took a few minutes for the next text to come, but he couldn't help but smile after reading it.

-I missed you too. Goodnight.

He walked downstairs to his home office and sent his list and the photo of the car to Ethan.

When he walked into Manhattan Nights, he was happily surprised to see that the place was packed. He loved it when the restaurant was booked for a party. Most of his staff was on hand that night so he stood back and watched each one to see if there was a hint of who might be the mole.

Ethan was running an extensive background search on everyone who had recently been hired or fired. He said it would take a few weeks to get any results. Trent doubted he'd find anything since he'd run the standard search on everyone he'd hired. The only employee he could remember having an issue with was Shane Cato. The ex-employee had been caught drinking. When Trent had confronted him, the man had gotten violent enough that he'd had to call the police to have him physically removed. But that had been almost a year ago and Trent hadn't heard or seen him since. Regardless, he'd put his name down on the list he'd sent to Ethan.

By closing time, Trent had a list of notes he'd taken after carefully watching each employee. Before letting anyone leave for the night, he called a meeting in the main dining hall.

"Thank you, everyone, for staying a little late. I promise this won't take long. As you all know, we've been getting some bad publicity. But after tonight, I'm reassured that Manhattan Nights is a finely oiled machine. However, I did want to call out a few items I think we can improve on." At this point, a few people groaned, but he ran through his list quickly and even had a couple employees make suggestions about what they thought could be improved. Several of the ideas were good enough that he implemented the changes on the spot.

Two of those ideas had been made by Angie. Trent was happy to see her stepping up again.

When he finally dismissed the crew, he walked to the back office and looked over the schedules, making a few changes here and there.

The lights were shut off when he walked back into the kitchen. He was shocked to see Angie waiting for him in the parking lot.

"I thought you would have gone already," he said as he started walking towards her.

"No, just thought I'd wait around for you to see if you wanted to grab a coffee."

He sighed and thought of his early meeting with Marina.

"Wish I could, but I have an early meeting in the morning." He looked down at his watch and cringed knowing he'd only get a few hours' of sleep. "I'm already a few hours shy of sleep."

She smiled. "I understand. How's the second site coming along?"

He smiled. "Great. You should swing by sometime. They've just put in the walls. Mind you, there's no ceiling yet." She smiled.

"Maybe you can show me around sometime."

He nodded. "I guess it would be helpful to have your thoughts on the kitchen." He planned on letting his employees decide which site they wanted to work at once Manhattan Nights II was finished.

"Well, I'd better let you get some rest." She opened her car door. "Good night." She stood there for another second then got behind the wheel.

When his alarm went off the next morning, he was feeling under the weather. When he stood, everything spun and he had to sit back down. He hated being sick. He took a little longer in the shower, downed a couple aspirin, and pulled on a long-sleeved shirt to ward off the chills that were shaking his body.

When he arrived at the coffee shop, he was drenched in sweat. Marina sat in the corner and frowned when she saw him.

She stood and reached up to feel his forehead. "You're burning up." She reached down and grabbed her bags. "Why on earth didn't you call me and cancel?"

He frowned. "I wanted to see you. You canceled yesterday, and this is the last time I can see you before you leave."

She tugged him out of the coffee shop. "Well, that's sweet." She looked up at him and smiled. "But I'm taking you home right now and putting you to bed." She started pulling him down the street then stopped. "That came out wrong."

He smiled for the first time, which almost caused his head to explode. He groaned and grabbed it. "How can this hurt so bad?"

"It's going around. It took Tommy all day yesterday to finally start feeling better."

He groaned, thinking of spending a whole day sick in bed. Then he remembered what she'd said—she was coming back to his place with him. Maybe this wouldn't be such a bad thing after all.

When he unlocked his front door, she marched him upstairs to his room. He watched her glance around quickly.

He'd spent a lot of money on the interior decorator and the place had come out perfect. It was a great mix of modern meets wood. It wasn't too masculine that a woman wouldn't feel comfortable staying over. Yet, he didn't feel like he was living at his mother's place.

"Nice space," she said as she motioned for him to sit on the bed. "Now, did you take something?"

He nodded his head and closed his eyes when the motion made him feel off-balance.

"Try not to move around. Tommy got sick every time he did."

"Great." He groaned and leaned back against the headboard.

She bent down and removed his tennis shoes. "You rest here, and I'll make you some tea."

"Tea?" He groaned again.

"Hmmm, maybe not yet. Rest." She pushed him back lightly against the headboard.

"It might help if you crawled up here with me," he said smiling slightly.

She smiled back. "Later. Rest now. I'll just go make up some soup for later."

He closed his eyes and groaned again at the thought of food. He fell asleep for a while, and when he woke, his stomach was doing turns, and there was a coat of sweat over his skin. He lunged out of bed and made it into the bathroom just in time to lose the contents of his stomach.

After showering, he started feeling a little better. He could smell something cooking and smiled when his stomach didn't revolt at the thought of food.

Taking the stairs quietly, he walked into the living room and was happily surprised to see Marina resting on his couch. She'd removed the silver heels she'd been wearing and had tucked her legs up underneath her skirt. Her arms were crossed, causing her breasts to push up higher and making him wish he could feel them against his chest. Her dark eyelashes looked sexy as they rested on her cheeks. Her lips were in a slight pout as she dreamed. Leaning down next to her, he ran his fingers over her cheek as he pushed a strand of hair away from her forehead.

He knew she might be the reason his business had been suffering the last few months, but he couldn't deny the attraction he felt for her. She was something more than he'd ever experienced, he just didn't know what, yet. But he was sure of one thing—he wanted more time to understand what was growing between them and the first step was right in front of him.

MARINA WAS FINISHING her dream from the previous night. The soft sand was pushing against her back, and Trent's hands were roaming over her body as she moaned with the pleasure he was giving her. His mouth was hot on hers and when she opened her lips, she tasted the minty zing of his tongue against hers.

His fingers ran through her hair, holding her still as he explored her lips and mouth. She felt his body come over hers as he moved slowly against her. She could feel the hardness in his jeans against the softness of her stomach. She wished that their clothes would disappear like they always did in her dreams, but for some reason, she couldn't will it so.

It took her foggy mind a few moments to realize why—she was no longer dreaming. Opening her eyes slowly, she smiled when she saw his blue eyes smiling back down at her.

"Hello." He pulled back, using his arms to hover over her.

"Hi." She smiled. "Did you sleep well?"

He nodded. "You?"

She nodded.

"You could have come up and crawled in bed with me," he said, running a finger down her cheek.

Her smile faltered.

"We can't fight it for long." His smile fell away as his eyes ran over her face. "This attraction we have."

She nodded, not sure if she trusted her voice. She'd had something for him for too long to deny it—seeing him run almost every day, the nightly dreams she'd had about him undressing her slowly. She felt like she was the one burning up now.

"Marina let me take you upstairs." He leaned down and kissed her again. "Let me peel that sexy dress from your body and worship it for hours." He ran his mouth down her neck and she felt herself shiver at the excitement.

She couldn't help but moan when his hands ran down her shoulders and cupped her slight breasts gently.

"Is that a yes?" He chuckled as he continued to kiss her. She couldn't stop herself from nodding.

He pulled back and smiled at her, then pushed himself off the couch and leaned down to pick her up.

"I can walk." She felt light-headed as he easily carried her towards the stairs.

"Where's the fun in that?" He chuckled. By the time they got to the top of the stairs, he was breathing hard.

"Maybe I'm still a little weak from the flu."

She nodded. She'd been breathing hard as well, but it was the anticipation of what was coming up next that had her breath hitching.

He carried her back into his bedroom, stopped just inside the door, and slowly slid her down until her feet rested next to his. She realized then that she no longer had her heels on and that he towered over her. She liked looking up into his crystal blue eyes. She could smell the fresh shower on him but saw that he hadn't shaved. The dark stubble on his chin made his light eyes stand out more. She ran her hands in his damp hair as he kissed her. When he started moving back towards the bed, she ran her hands down until she gripped his shirt and started tugging it over his head.

"I want to see you," she said against his lips. She'd dreamed about running her hands over that sexy body since the first time she'd seen him running without a shirt on.

He stepped back and yanked his shirt off over his head. Her eyes raked over him, leaving out no detail. He was beautiful.

When he stepped towards her, she felt a flash of nervousness.

"My turn." He smiled and started to open the buttons on her white silk shirt. She wore a tank top underneath. He slowly started pulling it up over her head and smiled when finally, she stood before him in only her white bra.

They looked at one another for a while, and then he reached out his fingers and brushed the back of his hand over her shoulder and down her chest until he cupped her. Her eyes slid closed and her head fell back with delight.

"So soft. So beautiful."

When his hand fell away, she opened her eyes, then stepped closer to him and reached out to touch his chest. His skin was soft over his hard muscles. His pecs and lats were impressive; she could spend the entire day exploring him. When she reached for his jeans, he chuckled and took her hands in his.

"Let's go slow. We have time." He stepped up to her again and placed soft kisses along her chin.

He moved them back again until she hit the edge of the bed. When his fingers moved around to undo the snap on her bra, she felt the flutter in her knees and was happy when he finally removed the barrier.

His mouth moved downward, and she groaned when his lips finally closed over her sensitive skin. Her fingers gripped his hair as he played his tongue over the tight nub.

His hands traveled down her sides, pushing her skirt down her hips until finally her silk skirt and panties lay in a pile at her feet.

When he stepped back and looked at her, she felt nervousness creeping in again. Her hands started to shake as she reached for his jeans again. This time, he nodded and smiled as she pulled open the button and slowly unzipped them. She pushed them over his narrow hips and groaned as he sprang free. It had been too long since she'd enjoyed a man. He stepped out of his jeans and stood there for her to view.

He was perfect. She looked at him and then realized he was looking at her, too. Heat caused her skin to flush as she stepped closer to him and brushed her body against his.

This time he moaned with pleasure. Then his lips were on hers and they were tumbling back onto the soft mattress. The air was knocked out of her lungs momentarily. Then he reversed their positions as his hands ran over every inch of her exposed skin.

He rained kisses along her shoulders, down over her breasts and ribs until he reached her navel and kissed a path across her hips. His fingers dug into her hips, holding her still as he lapped at her skin. Her hips pumped as his fingers brushed lightly over the soft curls that covered her sex. She could feel the moisture growing and wished more than anything to have his hands on her there.

"Please," she begged him as he avoided touching her in the one place she desired most.

"You're so soft," he said, as he looked down at her skin, his fingers gently rubbing over her curls. When he moved down and touched her, her shoulders jumped off the mattress as he explored every dip, every curve.

He shifted, and her eyes flew open as his mouth touched where his fingers had just been. She lost all thought as he explored her, pleased her.

Just when she thought she couldn't handle anymore, he moved up over her.

"Tell me you want this as much as I do," he said. When she nodded, he leaned over and pulled out a condom from his nightstand. Then he was kissing her again. "Tell me how much you want this."

She couldn't deny him. As he kissed a trail across her skin, she told him how much she'd wanted him all this time.

How she'd dreamed about him touching her, kissing her, making love to her.

He slid slowly into her as his blue eyes watched hers. A slow smile crossed his lips as he watched her eyes closed with pleasure. When he started to move above her, she couldn't control the shiver of pleasure that raced through her entire body.

When he started to move quicker, she lost all other thoughts except him.

rent listened to Marina's heartbeat as he tried to settle his own jumping pulse. Marina's hair floated around his face. Her soft scent around him caused his mind to focus on only his need for her.

When she stretched, pushing her soft breasts closer to his chest, he couldn't stop himself from wanting her again. His mind kept screaming at him that this was wrong, that she could be his enemy or could at least be working with his enemy. But his body wanted her over and over.

"Mmm," she moaned as her hands ran over his arms and chest. "I can't believe how good it feels to just lie around. It must be close to lunchtime now." She moved to get up, but he held her still.

"Don't move. I'm enjoying this too much."

He heard and felt her chuckle, and then she moaned as his hands got back to work moving over her. He felt little bumps rise over her. He started kissing them away and then took her again slowly. When he entered her, her eyes went dark and she moaned his name. Her lips were too soft not to kiss, her skin too scented not to taste; he was quickly losing his self-control. He tried to get himself under control, but he was enjoying every second of it, more than he'd ever enjoyed being with anyone else.

He realized he'd been thinking too much when she quickly flipped over and straddled his hips. When she leaned over, her breasts brushed against his chest as his hands reached up and cupped her gently. She smiled, which caused her beautiful dimples to flash quickly.

"Maybe you're still a little too sick to finish the job, so just lie back and let me nurse you back to health," she whispered into his ear. Images of her in a tight white outfit with a stethoscope around her neck flashed into his head. Then she started moving over him and he lost his train of thought as she used her hands and hips to bring him to his breaking point.

He slept for a while and when he woke up, he was alone in his bed. Hearing the shower running, he made his way into the bathroom and smiled when he saw her outline in the foggy shower door. He stepped in behind her, and she moaned as his hands ran over her wet body.

"I thought you'd gone," he whispered next to her ear.

"Soon. I have to get Tommy and pack for our trip." She turned and wrapped her arms around his shoulders.

"I wish you could stay longer," he whispered against her skin. When she moaned in response, he smiled, knowing she was thinking the same thing.

Half an hour later, he watched through a light rain as she jumped into a cab. He decided he was still not up to sitting at his computer and walked over to flip on a game on his large flat-screen television.

He fell asleep and when he woke, it was dark in the room. It took him a few minutes to figure out what was different. His TV screen was off and there was a blanket over his shoulders and lap.

Reaching over, he flipped on the light at the end of the couch. Frowning, he looked down at the blanket he swore he'd last seen in his hall closet. It was tucked over him with care. His television set was turned off and the remote was sitting over on the bar countertop, causing him to jump up, every muscle in his body on alert.

After spending ten minutes walking through his place, making sure everything was secure and he was really alone, he decided that he must have been sicker than he thought. There was no way someone would have broken into his place, turned off his television, and covered him with one of his grandmother's afghan blankets.

Walking back upstairs, he jumped into the shower and soaked away the last aches and pains of the twenty-four-hour bug before heading out to check on how things were running across the street.

By the next morning, he was up jogging like the flu hadn't hit him the day before. Instead of taking his normal jogging path, he ran past Marina's building without even realizing he was doing it. He would have continued except he almost knocked over a little red-headed boy that was trying to carry a large bag to a waiting taxi.

"Oops, sorry, buddy." He grabbed the little boy by his shoulders to steady him.

"S'okay." The boy looked up at him and smiled, flashing a set of dimples that looked familiar.

"Here, let me get this for you," he said, reaching for the bag.

"I can get it." The boy tried to pull the bag back, but it was too heavy for him and he started to fall again. Trent chuckled and easily took the bag.

"Maybe you should let your dad carry this out for you." He started walking to the taxicab, the boy on his heels.

"I don't have one. Besides, I'm a big boy now; I just turned eight last month." The little boy's chest puffed up and Trent could see his cheeks turning pink with anger.

"Wow," he stopped and knelt down. "Eight, huh?" When the boy nodded and something close to pride flashed in his eyes, Trent couldn't help but smile. "Well, then, I guess you are old enough to grab your own taxi then." Trent turned around and handed the bag to the waiting cab driver.

The boy chuckled behind him. "I'm not alone, my aunt is with me. See, here she is now." The boy nodded to the old stone building. When he turned around, he was a little surprised to see Marina standing in the doorway, two large bags in her hands and a very angry look on her face. It took her a second to finally step down the stairs and walk towards them.

"Mari, this man helped me carry my bag out. I could have done it myself, though." The boy frowned up at him.

"I'm sure you could have. Tommy, would you go sit in the cab and wait for me, please?"

Tommy nodded and skipped to the back door of the cab.

"You have some nerve," she said, shoving the bags towards the cab driver, almost knocking him over.

"What? Helping a kid with a bag that was too heavy for him to carry in the first place?"

"No." She turned on him and motioned with her hands. "Following me. Tracking me down. Like some kind of"—her hands flailed about— "stalker."

"Whoa, hold it now." He took her shoulders and walked her a few steps away from the taxi, so the little boy and the cab driver wouldn't hear their conversation. The fact was, he felt like a stalker. He knew he had to make things right with her, at any cost. "You have the wrong idea here. I was jogging along when I almost tripped over the boy. Honest, I had no idea he was your nephew. I swear."

He watched the anger drain from her face as she realized

he was in his normal jogging attire, with his ear buds hanging around his neck and his music blaring through them.

"Oh." Her mouth puckered in the sweet way he loved as she realized her mistake. "Oh, no. Trent, I'm so sorry." He felt her shoulders dip with embarrassment.

He chuckled. "Don't worry about it. So"—he nodded— "at least I finally get to see where you live."

She nodded, keeping her eyes down. He put his fingers under her chin and lifted until her eyes met his.

"He's a cute kid." He smiled as she nodded.

"It's just that I'm so protective of him. I wasn't sure I was ready for you two to meet."

He nodded. "Well, now that we have, maybe you won't be so hesitant about it in the future."

She nodded and smiled slightly.

"Good, so you'll bring him to the game on Thursday night?"

She nodded and smiled. "We better get going. We were running late as it was." She nodded towards the cab.

"Okay, but there is one more thing." He pulled her close and kissed her deeply right there on the sidewalk. When he felt her heart skip next to his, he released her. "There, now you can go." He smiled down at her when he saw that her eyes were cloudy and full of desire.

She nodded and licked her lips. His eyes followed the slow motion.

"Hurry back," he whispered to her when she turned to get into the cab. She nodded again.

MARINA SAT on the train heading to Boston and wished more than anything that she could get Trent out of her mind. But that kiss had clouded her vision and made her think only of him. She had a funny feeling that that had been his intention all along.

She'd been so upset when she'd walked out of her apartment and seen him kneeling down next to Tommy. At first, she'd yelled at herself mentally for allowing a man she hardly knew to get this close to her. She'd feared that she'd jeopardized everything that mattered most to her. But after she'd realized that he was wearing his jogging clothes, she relaxed a little. After all, it wasn't impossible that he'd run by her place before. There were only a dozen or so blocks between his place and hers and she didn't know how far he jogged on a regular basis.

"Mari, can Brian and I go to the food cart?" Tommy asked, breaking into her thoughts of Trent.

"Sure, let me grab my purse." She bent down to retrieve her bag.

"No," her nephew sighed. "We can do it all by ourselves."

The look the two of them gave her was priceless. But she shook her head no.

"What kind of chaperone would I be if I let you two wander the train all by yourselves? You wouldn't want Miss Keith to fire me now, would you?"

The boys looked at each other and shook their heads vigorously.

"Good, let's go then." Tommy was doing more each day to prove to her that he was growing up. He'd begged her that morning to carry his large bag down the stairs and out to the cab himself. She hadn't been concerned since she was just a few steps behind him but allowing him and his friend to roam the large train was different. She wasn't at the point where she could allow that. The way she felt about him, he would be in his thirties before she allowed him to walk to the corner by himself.

She smiled as they sat back down after getting a snack. The train was full of business people and a few families. When she looked around the car, she found her eye's zeroing in on a large, bald man. She'd bumped into him at the station and now she gave him a weak smile as he stared at her across the small space. When he didn't respond, she continued to eat her yogurt and read the book she'd brought along for the almost four-hour train ride. Since boarding almost two and a half hours ago, she'd hardly read a page. Either the kids were demanding her attention, or her mind was consumed by Trent.

Thinking about Trent, her mind sidetracked again, and the next time she surfaced, the train was pulling into the Boston station.

The next two days were a blur. The kids were a handful, but a complete joy. They went to the museums, the zoo, and even took a tour of Fenway Park. She'd been too busy to think about Trent, except when he would text or call her in the evenings.

They still had a full day to go and the small group was ordering pizza for lunch when she felt the small hairs on the back of her neck stand up. Glancing around, her eyes scanned the small Italian diner. She'd just about decided it had all been in her head when she spotted a familiar face outside the large windows.

Quickly grabbing Rebecca's hand, she asked for a moment and excused herself.

Walking out onto the street, she came face to face with Tommy's father. She'd known that he still lived in Boston, but not in a million years did she expect to run into him on this trip, or ever again. His deep red hair was styled away from his square features, so much like Tommy's. He wasn't a tall man, but the suit made him look powerful. Even for a man in his late fifties, he looked in great shape.

"Hello, Brandon. How did you find me?"

"I have my ways." He smirked then added, "Have you seen your sister?" He reached out and grabbed her arm tightly.

If anyone were to look at the scene, they would only see a US Congressmen standing on the corner casually talking to a woman. But his fingers were like a vice on her upper arm, causing pain to shoot throughout her body.

"Let go of me this instant," she said, calmly.

When he tightened his grip, she whispered, "I'd hate to make a big scene." She nodded around the crowded street.

When he dropped his hand, she rubbed her upper arm and sighed. She supposed she'd have to deal with this sooner or later.

"No, I haven't seen or heard from Trina in over a year." She looked up at him with fire in her eyes. "Though, if I had, I wouldn't tell you."

He glared at her. "I suppose that's the brat she tried to pull off as mine." He nodded towards the large window where Tommy sat shoving a large piece of Canadian bacon and pineapple pizza into his face.

"That's my nephew, Tommy. And if you think you have a chance of taking him away now..." She took a step towards him. "You'll have to go through me first."

Brandon looked down and her and cracked a thin smile. "If only your sister had the gumption you do." He shook his head. "The kid's not mine. I want nothing to do with him, but your sister has something of mine and"—he reached down and grabbed her arm tightly again, pulling her close until their noses almost touched— "I aim at getting it back, at any cost."

Just then, Rebecca walked out. "Is everything all right?" she asked. Marina noticed that she'd dragged the waiter out front with her.

Brandon dropped her arm and stepped back. "Everything's fine. Just visiting an old friend." He nodded and turned to get into the back of a black sedan that was parked illegally in the street. "Be sure to tell your sister that I'll see her around," he said before ducking into the back seat.

Marina shivered and rubbed her bruised arm as she watched the dark car drive away.

"Was that Brandon Hughes? The US Congressmen?" Rebecca asked, standing next to her.

"Yes." She turned and looked at Tommy's teacher, who had turned and was now looking closely at Tommy through the window. Marina shook her head. "Please don't ask."

Rebecca placed a hand on her bruised arm. "Did he hurt you?"

Marina sighed and shook her head as she looked down at the arm. "It's only a bruise." She shook the woman's hand off lightly.

"If you want to talk about it, I'm here." She smiled. "Well, come on, I'm starved." Rebecca smiled and started walking into the diner.

Over the last three days, Marina had gotten to know Tommy's teacher pretty well, and she had gained a new respect for the woman. She even considered her a friend. Her opinion of her had grown even more after seeing how she had handled the situation with Hughes.

When they arrived back at their hotel, there was a note at the front desk for her. She quickly stepped aside and opened it.

Stay away from my husband. You think you can pawn that little brat off on us? I know who you are and I won't tolerate this kind of behavior. This is your last warning.

Silvia Hughes

Marina crumpled up the note and tossed it in the nearest trash can. She remembered Silvia Hughes. The older frail woman was a socialite, never a hair out of place, always wearing an Armani suit and diamonds. The senator and she had never had children and it had gone around the rumor mill that she'd been barren, especially since the news of Tommy and Trina had spread in all the papers.

She didn't know why Mrs. Hughes felt threatened about her husband talking to her, but since she'd never hoped to see the man again, it wasn't going to be an issue.

CHAPTER 9

Trent found it very hard to concentrate while Marina and Tommy were in Boston, but the deadlines that loomed over him caused him to stay busy. He spent half his time at the new site sorting out the workers there and the rest of his time at Manhattan Nights. The restaurant was finally recovering from Marina's bad review. The two large rooms in the back were booked solid for the upcoming holiday seasons, including several large wedding receptions. He knew that a bad review could make or break a restaurant, but it seemed that most of his clientele hadn't paid too much attention to what others thought, after all.

As he's always told his staff, his food spoke for itself. He'd spent the first two years after opening Manhattan Nights perfecting his specialty items. They boasted the tastiest roasted duck in town. It had his grandmother's secret apple dressing on top, something that had been handed down to him and him alone. He didn't even let his staff know the recipe. Instead, he came in three times a week and cooked up a large batch of it.

That sauce had won more awards than even he could

remember. His grandmother, Florence, had brought the recipe over from Sweden when she was a child. It had been handed down from daughter to daughter until he'd shown an interest in cooking instead of his sister Rachelle, who had a talent for numbers and accounting.

Along with the apple dressing, there were a handful of other recipes of his grandmother's that he used. In fact, there was a large book of them that he kept in his home safe. If it hadn't been for that book, he never would have had the idea of opening up a restaurant. He owed a lot to his grandmother and mother for encouraging him to follow his dream.

He was working on only a few hours of sleep and had just found out that he'd have to pull a full shift tonight. He'd woken early for a meeting with the foremen at the new site to work through an issue they were having with the ventilation system. After going back and forth with the man and the building inspector for almost an hour, he'd walked away with a growing headache.

Now, as he stood and looked at his busy kitchen, he wondered how he would get the strength to make it through the night.

About an hour into his shift, his cell phone rang. He didn't let his staff hold onto their cell phones during a shift, but he made an exception for himself. Walking into his office, he answered the call from Marina.

"Hi," he said as he sat down behind his desk.

"Hi. I hope I'm not disturbing you." Just the sound of her voice made him smile.

"No, not at all. How was the museum today?"

"Wonderful. Did you know they have this huge game of Operation? You remember that game?"

"Yeah, loved it as a kid."

"Well, there's this huge section called Grossology where we learned all about the human body. Tommy loved this thing called the burp machine." She chuckled, and he couldn't help smiling along. "How was your day?"

"Very long and boring, but much better now that I've heard your voice."

She sighed, and he could just imagine her eyes turning darker as she thought about him.

"Have you decided about the game yet?"

She sighed again. "Yes, I've already told Tommy we would go. You would have thought I had given him a new Xbox. I had no idea the kid was into baseball. When I asked him, he started talking to me about some of his favorite teams. I had no idea."

He smiled. "Sounds like a man after my own heart. What do you say that I pick you two up before the game? That way we can hit the pizza parlor after we win."

She chuckled. "So sure of yourself, are you?"

"Hey, when you got it, you got it." He smiled and leaned back in his chair.

"Sounds great." He heard a noise and she covered the mouthpiece. "Sorry, duty calls. Looks like one of the boys just broke a hotel lamp. We'll see you Thursday."

"I'll be there around four, in front of your building."

"Okay, goodnight."

When he walked back into the kitchen, his headache was gone, and he had a slight spring to his step. He didn't know why talking to her made him feel like he was in school again, but he didn't want that feeling to go away anytime soon.

"You look happier," Carla, his chef de partie, said when he walked out of the office. Several other staff members turned to look at him.

"Yeah, I guess my headache is gone." He smiled and went back to work.

When he finally dragged himself across the street just after two in the morning, his headache was back. His eyes were red and dry, and he felt like he had a layer of slime over every inch of him.

He was so tired, he almost missed the fact that the lock on his front door was busted. His door was cracked open just a little and several lights that he knew he had turned off were on.

Taking his cell from his pocket, he dialed 911 and took a step off his stairs. He knew better than to run into the place without thinking. One of his buddies in college had walked in on a burglary and gotten a two-night stay in the hospital for it.

By the time the police arrived, he was sure there was no one in the place. You would have to be an idiot to stick around in a place for over half-an-hour.

A second after the police had confirmed no one was lurking in his place, he went in to see what the damage was. Everything was destroyed. His furniture, his curtains, and his kitchen table had all been chopped up with an ax that was still lying on the floor next to the pieces. Some of his art was in shreds after being cut in long strips. His kitchen scissors were shoved deep into his leather recliner along with several deeper cuts.

His dishes were in pieces on his kitchen floor. When he walked up the stairs into his bedroom, he found a large burn on his bed and was thankful he'd spent the extra money on the flame-retardant comforter and mattress the salesperson had suggested.

"Whoo-wee, that was a close one," one of the officers said from behind him. "Could have lost everything."

"Yeah," he said under his breath, wondering why someone would destroy everything instead of stealing it. Even his large flat-screen televisions were shattered, most likely by the ax, since there were deep holes and cuts in the cases.

"Now why would someone want to get back at you?" the

man asked. Trent turned on him and realized it was a different police officer from before. This one was taller and a lot younger than the first two that had shown up.

He shrugged his shoulders and turned back to the room. "Good question."

MARINA STOOD at the train station and glanced over her shoulder for the fourth time. She was sure it was the same man from before. She held onto Tommy's hand a little tighter.

"Oww," Tommy said, trying to pull his hand out of hers. "You're holding me too tight."

"Oh, sorry." She released his hand a little as she glanced over her shoulder one more time. It was the same man from their train ride to Boston. The bald man stared at her, not even trying to hide the fact that he was watching them.

Then Brandon's words came into her head. *I have my ways.* So, this is how he'd known where she was. How long had this man been following them? She grew angry. How dare he hire someone to spy on them? Then she realized the significance of it all. She'd been hiding for the last year, and now it appeared that it had all been in vain. Brandon had no intention of taking Tommy. He wanted her sister. Maybe that's why Trina had continued to stay away?

They boarded the train and Tommy laid his head in her lap and slept as she thought about what she should do next.

By the time they finally arrived back in New York, she had come up with a plan. And the first thing she had to do was contact her sister. Somehow.

At a quarter to four on Thursday evening, she glanced at her reflection one last time in her mirror. She couldn't remember feeling this nervous ever before and didn't know why she was having a hard time of it now. After all, it wasn't as if it was their first date.

Just then Tommy rushed in wearing his old jeans and a baseball jersey she'd gotten him last spring when he'd told her he liked the colors. Smiling, she realized she'd been blind to the fact that the kid was crazy about the sport.

She knelt down in front of him and straightened his shirt. "Don't you look handsome?"

He looked down at his shoes. "I don't have baseball shoes." He frowned and gave her his best sad eyes.

"Well, maybe we can do something about that this weekend."

"Really?" His eyebrows shot up.

When she nodded, he threw his arms around her neck and hugged her.

"You're the best, Aunt Mari." He rushed from the room quickly, leaving her wishing that the hug had lasted a little longer.

They stood out front for a few minutes before she saw Trent pull up in a new silver Mustang. He pulled to a stop right in front of them and jumped out to open the door for them.

"Wow," Tommy said. "I've never ridden in a car before."

She chuckled. "You've ridden in lots of taxis before."

He looked up at her and sighed. "Yeah, but those aren't *real* cars." He dropped her hand and waved his hands towards Trent's car. "Not like this."

"The kid has a point," Trent said, smiling over at her as he held the door open. "Well, then you're in for a treat. This happens to be my first time driving a car," he said, leaning down and talking to Tommy, but not before giving her a quick wink to let her know that he was joking.

"Wow, really?" Tommy took the bait and jumped up and down. "Then we'll take the maiden voyage," he said as he jumped into the back seat, surprising her with his knowledge.

She chuckled. "That kid never stops amazing me." She shook her head and started to get into the car, but he stopped her and pulled her close. The kiss was quick but seared her to the bones.

"Hello." He smiled at her as he rubbed his hands over her arms.

"Hi." She couldn't have stopped the smile if she had tried. Once she was seated in the car, she reached around to make sure Tommy's belt was on. She noticed a dark sedan sitting right behind them and thought for a moment that she saw a bald-headed man at the wheel behind the dark glass.

"I hope you don't mind, but I have to pick up Joe on the way," Trent said as he got in.

"No." She turned around, forgetting all about the car behind them.

By the time the game started, Tommy was so excited, she was having a hard time keeping him on the bleachers.

"Can I go in the dugout?" he asked over and over, to which she had replied at least a dozen times, "Maybe after the game."

After the first ten minutes, Terry walked up and sat down. Her blonde hair was cut shorter and was curly.

"Hi, who's this?" She sat next to Tommy.

"Hi." Tommy held out his hand for her to shake. "I'm Tommy. I'm almost eight and have a loose tooth." He proceeded to show Terry, who chuckled and looked at the tooth with great care.

"You sure do." She smiled and nodded at Marina. "Looks like someone likes baseball." She pointed to his shirt.

"I love it. When I grow up I'm going to be in the MLB," he said matter-of-factly.

"Really?" Terry asked. "Do you see that large man over

there?" She pointed to another team member, who was currently playing second base.

Tommy shook his head.

"That's Kyle Christensen. He used to play for the Orioles."

"Wow." Tommy's eyes got huge and for the rest of the game, he watched the man very closely while the two ladies talked.

"He's cute," Terry said, nodding to the boy.

"Yeah, but a handful." They giggled.

Twenty minutes through the second inning, the rain started. Marina pulled out her umbrella and she and Tommy and Terry huddled as close together as they could until it got so bad, everyone sprinted for shelter. After ten minutes of crowding under the concession stands awning, the game was called.

When they jumped back into Trent's car, she sat back and watched the crowds pass as they walked on the wet sidewalks.

"Well, I hope you two are still hungry," Trent said as he pulled into a strip mall area.

"I'm starving," Tommy said from the back seat.

"Great, because they serve some of the best spaghetti here, aside from my own." He parked and turned towards Marina and smiled, and she felt her heart skip.

"So, you can cook?" she asked, smiling. She thought she saw something flash in his eyes, but it was gone as soon as it had appeared.

"I've been known to bang around a few pots and pans." He turned and looked at Tommy. "How about you?"

Tommy made a funny face and frowned, and then surprised them by saying, "Cooking's for girls." They both laughed.

CHAPTER 10

After watching the kid down a whole plate of spaghetti, he decided to make the kid portions at Manhattan Nights bigger. And maybe even add a dessert while he was at it.

"Does he always put away that much food?" he asked on their short drive back to her place. The kid had passed out the second he hit the back seat.

She chuckled and looked back at the sleeping boy. "Yeah. When I first started watching him, I thought for sure within the first month that he would be overweight." She shook her head and glanced at him. "Oh, to have that metabolism again."

He pulled into a parking spot just down the street from her door. "I'll carry him up." He jumped out. Since the rain had slowed to a light drizzle, she nodded and opened her umbrella to cover the sleepy boy as he carried him down the sidewalk and up the stairs outside her building.

He maneuvered through the narrow doors and then followed her down the hall towards the back stairs and up to the second floor. Their apartment was on the backside of the old building, one of the three on her floor.

She opened her door and held it wide for him to step in. The apartment was small. Really small. But he followed her as she walked down a narrow hallway towards the kid's bedroom.

His first thought on seeing the size of her place was that Tommy's room was going to be cramped and crowded. He was shocked when he saw that the kid's room was bigger than the living room and kitchen together. Everything was organized, and the floor was cleared of toys and clothes.

"Wow looks like the kid knows how to clean," he said softly as he laid the little boys limp body on the bed and stood back and watched Marina slip his shoes off gently.

"Number one rule," she said over her shoulder as she pulled the kid's damp jacket off him and tucked him into bed. "I normally don't let him sleep in his clothes, but I'll allow it this time." She stood and walked towards the door. He followed and flipped off the light she'd turned on before shutting the door behind them. "How about a cup of coffee?"

He shook his head. "Don't touch the stuff, but I'm sure you have a cup of hot chocolate around." He smiled and pulled her closer.

"I'll see what I can do." She leaned up on her toes and placed a kiss on his lips.

"Mmm," he said when she pulled away. "Sweet as honey. Just the way I remembered."

When she tried to pull away more, he held her still. "Just a little more." He took his time and explored every curve that he could get his hands on. He wanted more, but he knew that there was a little boy fast asleep just on the other side of the door.

He pulled back slowly, giving her time to recover. "Now how about that hot chocolate?"

She smiled, and he could tell she was a little unsteady on her feet. He felt the same way and as he sat in her small but highly organized living room, he wondered why he was still playing the game with her.

Sometime in the past few days, he'd come to the conclusion that Marina was not the root of his problems. There was no way she was on the take. He was still considering the possibility of her being blackmailed and he knew he had to find out.

When she sat down next to him, carrying a tray holding two cups full of hot chocolate with colorful marshmallows floating on top, he knew he had to try and find out as much as he could.

"What do you do, exactly?" He tried to sound casual as he took a sip from his cup. He watched fear shoot into her eyes, but it was quickly followed by something else. He might have described it as surrender.

"I'm a writer," she said quickly, taking a sip from her cup and crossing her feet underneath her.

"Yes, so you've said. But you don't write books." She shook her head. "You write for a paper?" When she nodded, he lifted his eyebrows, waiting.

"I write self-help articles." She cupped her hands around her cup and blew softly as steam floated out.

"Self-help? How to cook? How to clean?"

She nodded. "I have several of those." She chuckled. "Have you heard of Meddling Marci?"

He sat up a little. "You're Meddling Marci?" When she nodded, he whistled. "Wow, I'm sitting next to a celebrity." He watched her blush a little. "That article has been running for over five years." She nodded again. "Everyone in Manhattan wants to know who Marci is." She glanced at him and he chuckled. "Don't worry; your secret is safe with me." He set his cup down and then took her cup from her hands and set it next to his. When he pulled her close, she sighed and relaxed in his arms. "What other articles do you write?"

"Oh, I have a few about the organization."

He chuckled. "I can tell. I've never been in such a small place that felt so comfortable before."

She smiled and looked up at him. "Thank you. I have one I just started last year about kid-friendly places to visit in the city."

"I could see some benefit to that one." He watched her bite her lip and think about her next words.

"I also write as a food critic." He tried to act surprised.

"Food critic, huh?"

She nodded her head and sat up a little. "That one seems to get me in the most trouble though." She reached for her mug again. "You'd be surprised what some restaurants will do to get a good review."

"I can bet." He tried to sound casual, but she glanced at him. "Have you ever taken a bribe?" He knew the answer before asked the question.

She shook her head. "Of course not. It's one of the main reasons I write under a pseudonym. So they can't find me. Do you know, I actually had a pub owner show up at my doorstep at three in the morning, drunk? He tried to convince me that his pickle sandwiches weren't as bad as they were. He had a whole plate of the smelly things and tried to shove them in my door."

He looked down at her and could see the humor in her eyes. But he could see an underlying fear, as well.

"It must have been scary."

She sobered and looked down at the forgotten mug in her hands. Setting it down again, she continued. "It's the main reason I stopped listing my address and got a post office box."

He felt the tension in her and decided to lighten the

mood. Pulling her close, he put his finger under her chin and asked softly, "What other hidden talents do you have?"

She smiled slowly, then ran her hands in his hair and pulled him down for a kiss.

———

SHE COULDN'T HAVE STOPPED herself if she'd wanted to. His mouth and hands felt too good on her to pull away. His blue eyes had called to her as he looked down at her. When they closed on a moan, she left behind thoughts of time and place and let her body take over.

Her hands were shaking as she ran them through his hair, and her breath hitched every time he touched her bare skin. She'd trusted him with one of her most coveted secrets and somehow knew that it was safe to do so.

When his hands roamed under her shirt, she arched back to give him better access to the spots she dreamed of him touching. Her hands fumbled to unbutton his jersey as his warm fingers skated over her ribs.

"Mmm, you're so soft," he whispered next to her neck as he trailed kisses over her skin. He leaned closer as she pulled his outer shirt off his shoulders and sighed when she realized he was wearing a thin white T-shirt underneath.

When she started pulling at his shirt, he leaned back and pulled it over his head quickly. Putting her hands on his chest, she held him at bay, so she could get her fill of looking at him.

"You're so beautiful," she said under her breath.

He smiled a little and then reached over and started pulling up her shirt. Halfway up, he paused. "Is the kid going to wake up?"

She shook her head. "No, he's a sound sleeper. He'd sleep through a hurricane." She smiled and helped him pull her shirt over her head. When she heard him sigh with pleasure, all of the nerves disappeared.

"Perfect," he said just before he bent down and placed a kiss on her shoulder. "I've missed the taste of you."

Leaning her head back, she felt her world spin as he took his time tasting and nibbling her skin. Then he was pulling her up into his arms and carrying her towards the hallway.

"The last door," she said against his neck as she nipped at his ear with her teeth and tongue. She'd closed her eyes and let the feeling consume her as she felt herself being carried the short distance.

She heard her door shut and the lock button push in behind them, and then saw a bright light through her closed lids. When she opened her eyes, she had to blink a few times so her eyes would adjust.

"I want to see you." He smiled down at her. He was still standing just inside her doorway, looking down at her. His crystal eyes were roaming over her exposed skin. "Perfect," he said again, right before he took her mouth with his.

She felt herself sliding down his body, her warm skin against his. She felt the change when his hands and mouth turned hungry like her own had. She tugged at his uniform pants as his fingers yanked at her jeans. The rest of their clothes hit the floor and he started to walk her backward towards the edge of her bed.

She expected him to pull her down on the bed, but instead, he stopped and held her closer. "This is so wrong," she thought she heard him whisper. His eyes were closed, and he was resting his forehead against hers.

"Tommy won't wake up. Besides, you locked the door." She pulled him back to her. She felt his stiff shoulders relax a little as he sighed.

"Marina," he pulled back a little, but she was pulling him

back to her. She didn't want the feeling to stop; she didn't want him to stop. Not when she was heated up so much.

"Please, Trent. I want you, no, I need you." She dug her nails gently into his shoulders and turned him around, so his knees were now hitting the edge of her bed. Pushing slightly, she went down with him as they landed softly on her mattress.

When she pulled back to look down at him, her knees on either side of his narrow hips, he was smiling up at her.

"Well, since you put it that way." His hands were on her hips, digging in slightly. "There's a condom in my wallet." He nodded towards his discarded jersey.

She smiled. "I'm prepared." Reaching over, she pulled a string of them from her nightstand. He chuckled. Then she tossed them on the bed next to them and leaned in to take his lips with hers.

When his fingers ran over her skin, lightly pulling at her nipples, her hips started moving above him. He lifted his head and replaced his fingers with his warm mouth, using his tongue to send bumps all over her skin.

This time she wanted to explore him; she'd dreamed about it for the last few nights. She gripped his wrists in her hands and pulled them above his head.

"Last time, I didn't get to explore as much as you did." When he smiled, she nodded towards his hands. "Keep them up."

Then she let her fingers roam slowly down his arms, feeling every vein, every muscle until she touched his chest. His skin was soft over the hardness of his pecs. "You must work out a lot in addition to jogging." He nodded and closed his eyes to the pleasures she was giving him. Her fingers circled his flat nipples, and then she leaned down and trailed her mouth and tongue over the same path. He tasted salty and delicious. She sucked lightly on his nipple and she felt his shoulders flex on the mattress.

Pulling back, she noticed that there was a light dusting of soft, dark hair that led from his belly button to his erection. Using just her fingertips, she trailed the pathway and watched him respond to her touch.

When she gripped him lightly, his eyes flew open and he watched her from below his dark eyelashes. Smiling, she kept her eyes on his as she dipped her head and ran her mouth over the length of him. He watched her silently as she used her mouth to please him. She heard him open one of the foil packages above her and knew that she was too far gone to stop herself. Then she felt his fingers dig into her hips, and she was being tossed on the mattress. Her back bounced on the bed as he came over the top of her. In one quick motion, he plunged into her and growled.

"Too fast?" he asked next to her ear as his hips pumped faster. Her legs wrapped around his hips, pulling him closer, faster. She shook her head as her nails dug into his shoulders. She threw her head back and cried out his name.

"More?" he asked as she felt herself slide down.

"More," she repeated as he reached down with his fingers and found her taut slick nub. She felt her world explode in an array of light and her legs went weak just as he moaned her name next to her ear.

Sometime later, as his hand gently played over her bare shoulders, she opened her eyes and looked across the messy sheets at him.

"I'd better get going," he said.

She was too far gone to register that thought until his weight was being removed from the mattress.

"You could stay, you know," she said, sitting up next to him on the side of the bed.

He shook his head. "Better not. I've got an early meeting

tomorrow." He smiled and then leaned down and placed a soft kiss on her lips. "Maybe next time."

She watched him walk across the room and pull on his tight jersey.

"You know," she said, tilting her head and enjoying the view, "I could get used to seeing you in uniform."

He turned his head and smiled at her. "Then you'll come to our next game? You and Tommy?"

She nodded. Her thoughts of him had already heated her body again. She stood up and walked across the room towards him, completely naked. Wrapping her arms around his shoulders, she pulled him back towards the bed. "You don't have to leave right away, do you?"

He leaned down and placed a kiss on her lips, starting a few more fires under her skin.

He shook his head. "No, I suppose I don't," he said right before they fell back onto the bed.

CHAPTER 11

The next morning's meeting didn't sit well with Trent. Not only was the construction delayed on Manhattan Nights II, now it looked like some of the building permits had gone missing.

He was standing in front of the new building talking to the construction manager, Doug, when Jake Baird, the owner of Cario's, came out and waved him down.

"Hey, Trent." Jake walked up and shook his hand. "Heard you've been having some problems."

Trent looked around. "Problems?"

"Yeah," he said, frowning at Doug. "I thought he had told you."

Trent turned towards Doug. "Problems?"

Doug cleared his throat. "Nothing that I couldn't handle. Besides, you've been really busy with the other site."

"Uh," Jake said, taking a step back. "Well, um, I'll chat with you later. It's good to see that things are finally moving along," Jake said, making a hasty retreat.

"Problems?" Trent asked Doug again. Trent had known Doug for years. He'd actually gone to college with his brother, Mark. That's why he'd hired him to help at Manhattan Nights and now again for Manhattan Nights II.

"It was just some kids. They broke in and busted a few things. No biggie. Our insurance paid for everything and it only took a full day out of our schedule." Doug shrugged his shoulders.

"When was this?" Trent had a sinking feeling.

"Three nights ago. But, like I said, everything was back up and running the following business day."

"Tell me you called the police," he said, rubbing his temple as he felt a headache attacking quickly.

"Sure, that's standard. I have a copy of the report in my office. I didn't want to bother you since it was our equipment that was busted, and it was on our insurance. Listen, we get this kind of thing happening all the time, kids breaking into a site, tagging stuff." He motioned for Trent to follow him to a small trailer that was parked on the sidewalk a few feet away.

"Tagged? They spray-painted things?"

"Well, sure. You know how it goes. If it's a clear spot, kids will spray-paint on anything."

"What did they paint?" he asked, stepping into the small space. Immediately, he thought of Marina's small space and how Doug could benefit from her organization skills.

"Well," he said, digging through a pile of papers. "On the side of the crane, they tagged a few choice words and some-thing about someone's mother." He stopped and smiled. "The funny part was that they used one of our axes to slice up the dust plastic. It must have taken them over an hour to chop it all up. Since the building was locked up tight, the damage was limited to the outside. They did manage to tag up the plywood pretty good, but we replaced all that easily enough." He pulled out a piece of paper with NYPD at the top. "Here it is. They took pictures and everything and gave me a copy for my insurance claim. Already talked to the adjuster and received a check to repaint the crane and replace the plywood."

Trent sat down in the folding chair and looked over the paperwork. It was hard to tell if it was the same person who had attacked his place. But it was just too big of a coincidence, especially knowing that both places had been hit in the same night.

"Can I make a copy of this?" he asked Doug.

"Sure." He took the paperwork from him and stuck it in a small copier that sat behind his messy desk. "Like I said, nothing big. I didn't think of calling you since I knew you had your hands full already."

"I appreciate it, but from now on, let me know if anything like this happens again."

"Sure will," Doug said, handing him the copies. "Oh, if you want, I can email you the pictures I took on my phone."

"That would be great." He frowned down at the paperwork as he walked out.

He made it back to his place around noon and was highly disappointed that the cleaning crew was still removing all the broken pieces. It had taken them four days now to clear the debris that used to be his house.

Since he no longer had a desk or kitchen table, he sat at his bar on one of the barstools he'd carried across the street from the restaurant, working on his laptop. After only half-an-hour of sitting in it, he realized just how uncomfortable they were. He made a mental note to replace all of them the first chance he could.

He was punching away at his keyboard when he heard a gasp behind him. Turning around, he saw Marina standing inside his doorway, her jaw dropped and her eyes huge. She was wearing a dark blue sweater dress. She wore a light scarf around her shoulders that was tossed across her in a low dip. Her tall black heels made him want to get his hands on those long legs of hers. Her hair was tied up in a loose knot.

"What happened here?" she asked, not moving from the doorway. The workers continued to bang around as she stood there, shocked.

"Marina?" He got up from his stool and walked over to the door. "What are you doing here?"

She shook her head and held out a bag of food from one of his favorite Thai places down the street. "I thought I'd see if you were free for lunch." She handed him the bag without even looking at him. "Where you robbed?" She walked into his place and started looking around.

"Not really." He followed her across the room and set the food on his bar.

"You didn't do this yourself, did you?" She turned on him.

"Of course not." He chuckled. "I actually liked my furniture."

She turned around and almost bumped into a worker.

"Tell everyone to take an hour for lunch," he said to the worker and watched as the crew of four quickly left.

When they were finally alone, he pulled her close and kissed her slowly. No one had brought him lunch in years and the fact that she'd thought of him made him feel all soft inside.

"There, now my day is finally going better."

She smiled up at him. "Are you going to tell me what happened?"

He sighed. "Someone broke in and decided to take their anger out on my furniture."

"Did they destroy it all?" She looked towards the stairs and the back rooms.

"Afraid so. They even got my great-grandfather's clock."

"Oh, Trent. I'm so sorry."

He kissed her again. "Now that you're here, it's better." He backed her up until her hips hit the granite countertops. "Now tell me why you're really here," he said when he felt her heart skip against his hands.

He hoisted her up on the tall counter, and his hands roamed under her dress as he enjoyed her luscious lips, which had been painted a light shade of pink. "Mmm, cherry," he said, licking at her lips.

She smiled and wrapped her legs around him. His hands slowly moved down her soft legs until he was gripping her ankles. "I'm liking these heels."

"Boots," she said as she tried to pull him closer. He pulled back.

"Boots?" He looked down at the tall shoes. "Boots come up to here." He slowly ran his hand up her calf and stopped just below her knee. "Or up to here." He ran his hands up higher to her thighs, pulling her dress up higher. He watched her head roll back and was happy when a dark lock of her hair sprang loose.

He wanted his hands on the softness but decided to wait until he was done enjoying her legs. He moved his hands up higher until he came to a barrier. "Are you wearing garters?"

Her eyes opened, and a smile formed on her lips as she nodded.

"For me?" he asked, running his fingers over the soft material. She nodded again, and he couldn't control the smile. "You are in so much trouble," he said right before his lips crushed hers. Her hands pulled at his shoulders as his went even higher on her thighs. When he reached her soft curls, he realized that she wasn't wearing any panties and his mind flooded with desire so fast, he actually felt his head spin.

The next moment he was yanking his jeans down his hips and pulling her to the edge of the countertop. Before he could gain control, he was inside her and listening to her scream in delight. Her legs wrapped around his hips and held him close to her. She'd rolled her head back and he was delighted to see that most of her hair had come loose from the bun.

His eyes roamed over her; the sweater had strayed lower, giving him a beautiful view of those soft breasts. The scarf had fallen off her shoulders and one of the shoulders of the dress had followed. The skirt of the dress was hiked up over her hips, exposing every inch of them twisted together. He watched as he slowly exited her soft lips, then he flexed his hips and entered her again as her skin gave way to his. He watched the movements for a while until finally, he couldn't stop the speed he desired.

Placing his hand on her nether lips, he felt where their bodies combined. His other hand went to her lower back, holding her close to him as he thrust farther, faster.

When his eyes closed, his mind played over every detail of how wonderful she'd looked lying naked underneath him last night. How her breasts had looked as he'd kissed them, licked them…

When he opened his eyes again, he was happy to see that her left nipple was almost exposed through the loose material. Reaching around, he helped the sweater dip lower and pinched the bud lightly.

She was biting her lower lip, her arms wrapped around his shoulders as she held onto him. When he dipped his head to taste the sweetness of her, she leaned back, allowing him better access.

"Marina," he said, not quite sure what he had meant to say, but when her dark eyes opened, and she looked at him, he felt something different that he hadn't expected.

She shook her head. "No, don't slow down. Don't stop. Not now. Not when I'm so close." She squeezed her thighs, holding him tighter to her.

At that moment, he would have given her anything. Done anything to make her beg him some more.

His hips sped up, and his mind whirled, as he watched her tongue dart out and lick her bottom lip. His eyes lowered to her exposed nipple and he watched it pucker for his view.

Groaning, he tossed his head back and shouted her name as he felt her inner muscles tighten around him.

An hour later, he sat in his kitchen at his bar and tried to get the image of Marina with her dress hiked up out of his mind. They had hastily eaten the Thai food she'd brought. She'd left right before the work crew had returned from their lunch.

He had just gotten his mind clear and was working on approving some orders for the restaurant when his phone rang.

Smiling, he answered and stepped out on his balcony.

"Can't stay away from me very long, huh?" He smiled.

"Stay away from the bitch or she'll burn." The voice was low and garbled and put him instantly on alert.

"What have you done with Marina?" he asked, rushing back into the house and picking up his home phone.

"Stay away from her!" The scream was so loud, he had to pull the phone away from his ear as he dialed 911 with the other phone.

"Where—?" he started to say, but he heard a click and the line went dead.

MARINA LEFT Trent's apartment feeling like she was floating down the street. She was sure that everyone she passed could guess that she had just had mind-blowing, countertop sex with the man of her dreams. But she didn't care.

Her plan had worked. She'd never gone over to a man's

place and seduced him before. She had dressed for the purpose of stopping by his place. The garters had been a last-minute add that she was now thankful for.

On the way there, she had almost backed out several times. She'd stopped in a small Thai restaurant and it had taken all her willpower to finally leave with a to-go order and the courage to follow through.

When she finally got to her apartment, she was shocked to find a dozen cops standing outside the doorway. Police cars were blocking the road and there was a yellow rope blocking off the stairs. There must have been thirty people standing outside the barriers, watching what was going on.

Fear instantly jumped into her mind. "What's going on?" she asked someone standing next to her as she tried to push her way farther forward.

"A woman was kidnapped," the man said, keeping his eyes on the building.

Her mind flashed to an image of Julie. "Oh, no." She pushed harder. "Please, let me through. I live here," she said just as the crowd parted.

"Marina!" someone shouted. She turned and saw Julie running towards her. Instantly, she relaxed, knowing her friend was okay.

"You're okay?" she asked her as her friend hugged her tightly.

"Me? What about you?" Julie asked.

"I'm fine." She frowned at her friend. "Who was kidnapped?" She looked around the building.

"You, apparently," Julie said, motioning towards a rather large police officer. "This is Marina Jenkins and apparently she doesn't know that she's been kidnapped," Julie said, laughing.

"What?" Marina turned on her friend. Then her mind

sharpened. "Tommy!" She started rushing towards the school, only to have an officer stop her.

"We've sent a female officer to go get your son. She's on her way back here with him now." He took her arm and steered her towards the front doors. "If you don't mind, we'd like to straighten out a few things."

Just then, there was a loud squeal as Trent's car pulled up behind the barriers.

"Marina!" he shouted as he ran towards her. He rushed through the barrier, almost knocking down a skinny cop in his path. He didn't stop until she was in his arms. He said her name over and over again in her hair.

Fifteen minutes later, she sat in her small living room with Trent, Julie, and two of New York's finest investigators. Tommy was in his room, completely content to have gotten out of school for the rest of the day and extra excited that he had actually gotten to ride in a real police car. The female officer had even run the sirens and lights for him.

She and her partner were sticking around and playing with him in his room while Marina went over a few things with the investigator.

The first question had thrown her for a loop.

"Miss Jenkins, do you know the whereabouts of your cell phone?"

"It's in my purse," she said, reaching down to empty her handbag. But when she dumped the contents out, her phone was not there. "Well, it was."

"When was the last time you used your phone?"

"She called me from it around noon," Julie said, reaching over and taking her friend's hand.

"Yes, it was ten till and I was checking to make sure Julie was going to get Tommy today. We swap days now." She smiled over at her friend.

"Where were you when you called her?" the thin officer

asked. He had a large pad of paper on his lap and had written everything they'd been saying.

"I was on Fifteenth Avenue walking towards Jimmy's Take-out Thai place. I stopped off to get some lunch."

He nodded. "Good place, great food. Did you have your phone when you left Jimmy's?"

She thought about it. "I think so, but I'm not sure. I might have set it on the counter to pay."

The officer wrote down a few more notes. "Where did you go after leaving Jimmy's?"

She looked over at Trent. "To Trent's place."

The man wrote down some more notes and glanced at her. "How long were you there?"

She looked at Trent.

"A little under an hour. We had lunch together," he answered.

She felt her face heat, remembering what they had been doing.

The officer got Trent's address and asked, "Where did you go after leaving his place?"

"I walked straight home."

He nodded and jotted down some more notes.

"Do you know of anyone who would want to scare you like this?"

She thought about it and something came to mind. "I... I received a note from Mrs. Hughes when I was in Boston."

"What?" Trent's hand tightened on hers.

"What kind of note?" The officer asked.

She looked over at Trent and could see his eyes growing hot. "It said to stay away from her husband." She looked at the officer and quickly explained everything.

By the time she was done, Trent was standing at the window looking out. She could tell he was upset but knew that he now had the full story.

The police assured her that they would look into everything and get back to her. She doubted it though. As soon as she had started talking about the US Senator's wife, they had both looked at each other and the one taking the notes had actually flipped his notebook closed.

It was almost an hour later when everyone finally left her apartment. Everyone except Trent. She was happy when she overheard him telling the officers and Julie that he was staying the night.

CHAPTER 12

Trent stood in Marina's living room and looked out at the dark sky. He'd quickly driven back to his place and had grabbed an overnight bag while Julie had stayed with Marina.

On his way back to her place, he had called Ethan and asked him to renew his efforts to find out who was messing with him. He filled him in on what had happened.

"Have you thought that it might be someone from her past and not yours we should be looking for?" Ethan asked.

"Her past?" Trent hadn't thought of that angle.

"I'll look into it. In the meantime, what would you say to some extra protection?"

"I didn't know you were on the East Coast."

Ethan chuckled. "Nope, still in the great Northwest. I was thinking more along the lines of sending you a very large Jamaican."

After hanging up with Ethan, Trent couldn't stop thinking that maybe he'd been going at it all wrong. Maybe the person who had broken into his place was someone from her past instead of his. Did she have an ex that was stalking her? Maybe a crazed fan? He'd been able to track her down with some help; maybe someone else had done the same.

There were so many possibilities that by the time he had arrived back at her place, his head felt dull.

"You look tired," she said, walking up behind him and wrapping her arms around his waist.

"Busy day." He turned and placed a kiss on her forehead. "You really had me scared."

She nodded and lay her head on his shoulder. "I can only imagine."

"Tomorrow's Friday. Let's take Tommy out of school and spend the day together."

She pulled back, her eyes going narrow. "Why?"

"Isn't it enough to know that I want to spend the day with you and a seven-year-old?"

"I'm almost eight," Tommy said from the doorway. "Can we go to the zoo?"

Trent laughed. "Sure, I haven't been to the zoo in…"—he thought for a moment— "too long."

"Yippee, can we Mari? Please?" Tommy rushed across the room and joined the hug.

"Sure." She laughed as the three of them almost fell over. "The zoo sounds wonderful."

"Woohoo!" Tommy jumped away and started to climb on the couch.

"Oh, no, you don't." Marina rushed over and picked him up. "Last time you jumped up and down on my couch, you almost broke the springs." She tickled him, and he fell on the cushions in a fit of giggles.

"Can we have mac and cheese for dinner?" He sobered up after she stopped her tickle attacks.

"I was thinking turkey and green beans." Tommy made a funny face and proceeded to beg for his dish instead.

Trent stood along the glass windows and watched the

motherly display of Marina trying to argue with an almost eight-year-old.

In the end, they had homemade macaroni and cheese with green beans on the side. After Tommy was bathed, a process that Trent had lent a helping hand with, and the kid was tucked into his bed in his Batman pajamas, Trent and Marina settled down in the living room and watched television.

Halfway through the news, he felt Marina drift off. He watched the rest of the news then carried her into her room and lay next to her. His mind refused to shut down, so he listened to her breathe until he finally drifted off.

Something woke him a few hours later, and he lay there and listened, wondering what it had been. Then he heard the kid crying and gently moved Marina aside to walk into the next room.

When he walked into Tommy's room, the boy was sitting up in his bed. Turning on the low light, Trent walked over to him.

"Hey, what's all this?" He sat next to him.

"I had a bad dream." The boy pulled the covers over his lap. "I peed my bed," he said, looking down as his shoulders slumped.

"Well, that can happen," Trent said, putting his finger under the boy's chin until he looked up at him. "Don't worry about it. I'm sure Marina has some clean sheets around here."

"I'm not a baby," Tommy said, his small lower lip quivering.

"Of course, you aren't. You're almost eight. That's practically a man."

Tommy's eyes got bigger. "It is?"

"Well, sure." Trent hoisted the kid off the wet sheets. "I remember when I was eight. That's the age when a lot of things change for boys. I remember getting picked for my first baseball team. I was no longer on the t-ball team. That was for kids." He stood the boy up and started to peel off the wet pajamas. "I was old enough to walk to the bus stop at my corner all by myself. Of course, my mom always watched from the front steps." He smiled as the little boy nodded.

"Mari lets me walk to the corner by myself now."

He nodded and then continued. "I also had a couple things going on with my body." He sobered. "Every time I had a nightmare, I had to go to the bathroom."

"You did?" Tommy asked as he pulled on a clean nightshirt.

Trent nodded. "Do you know how I solved it?"

Tommy shook his head as he stepped into some new night shorts.

"I forced myself to go to the bathroom each night before I hopped into bed."

"Did it work?"

He nodded and smiled and then started to pull off the soiled sheets. Tommy rushed over and helped.

"My mom bought me a special night-light." Trent nodded towards the baseball night-light that was right by the kid's closet. "Kind of like that one. It helped make all my night-mares go away."

"Mari bought that one for me last week after she found out I liked baseball."

Tommy rushed over and pulled out some clean sheets from his bottom drawer. "Here, these ones are my backup sheets." He set them on the bed. "You can put those in my hamper." He pointed to a large hamper just inside his closet door.

When Trent had the bed remade, he pulled the blankets up around Tommy and sat next to him. "You okay now?"

Tommy nodded. "Thanks, Trent. Night." He turned over and snuggled down in his clean sheets.

When Trent stood to go, he noticed Marina standing in the dark doorway, smiling at him.

He put his finger over his lips, took her hand, and walked with her back to her room.

"You were great with him," she said, walking into his arms and placing a soft kiss on his lips.

He shrugged his shoulders. "He's a good kid."

"You're a good man," she said back, placing another kiss on his lips as she pulled him back onto the bed.

He woke the next morning with an almost-eight-year-old bouncing on his chest.

"Come on, get up," he heard. When he cracked open his eyes, Tommy leaned closer to his face. Both of his small hands rested on either side of his scratchy face. The softness of them was his undoing.

"Why should I get up?" he asked, smiling into the dark eyes.

"'Cause we're going to the zoo. Mari has already made breakfast and you just have to get up." The boy started tugging on him, trying to push him along faster.

Trent chuckled. "I'm going to need a lot more convincing. What's your aunt cooking for breakfast?"

"Banana pancakes." He smiled. "My favorite."

Trent sat up quickly, almost dislodging the kid in the process. "Mine too." He grabbed Tommy and tucked him upside down under his arm and walked quickly into the kitchen area. Marina was standing at the stove, a spotless white apron on. Her hair was tied back in a high ponytail, making her look younger and very fresh. He walked over to her, Tommy still tucked under his arm and placed a kiss on her lips. "This kid here says you have homemade banana pancakes somewhere in here."

Tommy's laughter was priceless as Trent turned him right side up and sat him in his chair. He sat next to him at the table and waited for Marina to bring in a large plate of pancakes.

After three full helpings of some of the best pancakes he's had since his mother used to cook for him, he showered and got dressed quickly.

As they walked to the zoo, Tommy held his and Marina's hands. He talked nonstop about what kind of animals they were going to see and how the bald eagle was his favorite animal.

"Because it's our freedom," he explained, making Trent proud of the kid. "Course, I like the monkeys, too." He looked up at him with a smile. "They always make me laugh."

"Me, too," Trent agreed.

"I like the giraffes the best," Marina said, swinging Tommy's hand slightly. "They are so majestic."

When they got there, there was a large group of kids all wearing the same brightly colored shirts.

"School day visits," Marina explained. "But, most of them follow the tour guides." She nodded towards some staff members who were trying, along with the help of a few teachers, to get all the kids heading in the right direction.

"We can either follow them or head this way." She nodded towards the left.

He smiled. "Let's set our own path today. Tommy, where to first?" he asked, kneeling down while the boy opened the zoo map he'd handed him.

"Well…" Tommy's face squashed up a little as he looked at the map. "We are here." He pointed to the entrance. "They are heading to the monkeys." He pointed to the large group. "We can go here, to the polar bears first."

"Sounds like a plan. Lead the way, little man." He stood up and held onto Tommy and Marina's hands as they walked.

For the next two hours, Tommy led them around the zoo, sometimes even in circles, but he and Marina didn't mind.

When it was lunchtime, they sat at a cart vendor and had hot dogs and sodas followed by ice cream cones. An hour after lunch, they noticed that Tommy was slowing down, so Trent picked him up and carried him on his shoulders until they made it back to the apartment.

That evening, they rented one of Tommy's favorite movies. As the Lego characters ran around on the screen, Trent couldn't stop thinking about how everything just felt right.

He knew he had to come clean with Marina about who he was, but he didn't want anything to spoil the perfect time they were having. So he kept his mouth shut and packed the weekend days with as much fun as he could come up with. The nights, he spent making love to Marina or lying in bed holding her as his mind yelled at him to tell her the truth.

By Sunday afternoon, he had come up with a few dozen questions he needed to ask her before heading back to work on Monday afternoon. After Tommy was tucked in his bed, excited to go back to school the next day to tell all the kids about his weekend, he pulled Marina into the living room and sat down next to her on the couch.

"I know we've avoided talking about some things this weekend," he said, running his hand over hers. She nodded her head. "Can you think of anyone who would want to hurt you or Tommy?"

"I've been thinking about it all weekend." She sighed and rested her head back. "Tommy's father is a pretty high-powered man. But I ran into him in Boston, and I don't believe he even cares to acknowledge his existence."

"Is his father Brandon Hughes?" Trent asked, already knowing the answer.

Marina didn't seem surprised that he knew. Nodding her head, she continued. "Yes. My sister Caterina and he had an affair when he and his wife were separated. But he has yet to acknowledge that Tommy is his. At one point he demanded a blood test, which I ended up paying for."

"What were the results?" He watched her eyes flare, but she sighed, and they went back to looking tired.

"He's Tommy's father. My sister is a screw-up. Has been since puberty. But she's no liar, at least not when it comes to things like this. Brandon insisted on more tests, claiming that he was being framed. He even tried to have Trina arrested." She shook her head. "My sister was—is—still probably going through addiction. I think the smartest thing she's ever done was leaving that kid with me." He watched as a tear escaped her closed eye. Gently, he leaned in and brushed it aside.

"He has a good aunt. No one could contest that he's well taken care of and loved."

She nodded her head and looked at him. "Brandon did mention that my sister had something of his and that if I see her again to tell her he needs it back." She frowned.

"Something? Did he say what it was?" She shook her head and he made a note to pass that information on to Ethan.

"What about ex-boyfriends? Someone from your work?"

She looked at him, a slight frown on her lips. "You mean like a stalker?" When he nodded. "I might have pissed a few people off in my line of work, but I don't think anyone knows who I really am. I'm very careful with my identity."

"How did Hughes find you?"

She frowned. "I think he's had me followed for a while. There's a thin bald man that I've seen around a few times."

He tried to control his anger. "Someone has been following you and you're just now telling me?" He took a deep breath.

She nodded and shrugged her shoulders. "I'm very careful."

"Yes, so you've said." He stood up and started pacing in the small space. "Okay," he said after a few moments of silence, "new rules. You don't go anywhere alone, at least for the next few weeks. Tommy doesn't go anywhere alone. I'll move some more of my stuff over here—"

"Now wait just a moment." She stood and stopped him from pacing by stepping in front of him. "I won't sit here and be dictated to like I have no say in my life. I have a job to do, and I can't go around dragging someone along with me. I've never let Tommy go anywhere by himself, and I'm not about to start." She pushed a finger into his chest, and he felt his respect for her growing for standing up for herself. "Besides, maybe I don't want you moving in. Last time I let someone move in with me it didn't turn out so great." She crossed her arms over her chest and frowned at him.

He pulled her close and kissed her until he felt all the tension leave her body. Pulling back a little, he rested his head on hers. "I don't want anything bad to happen to you two. Please, let's just try it my way for a while."

She sighed and rested her hand over his heart. "Fine. I guess I can reschedule some of my appointments and see if Julie could tag along with me."

He ran his hand through her hair. "Thanks. How about using those organization skills and making some more room in this place for some of my things?"

She looked up at him and laughed.

CHAPTER 13

Over the next few days, Marina stayed very busy. She'd had a lot of work to catch up on since her trip to Boston, not to mention taking the whole weekend off with Tommy and Trent.

She sat at her small desk and tried not to sigh, thinking of how wonderful the weekend had been. Maybe she was fooling herself into believing Trent felt the same way, but she couldn't deny how much fun Tommy had had with him. He would make a wonderful father.

She looked up at her small mirror and frowned. What was she doing? She'd never really thought about having kids before. Especially after she had started watching Tommy full-time. But now an image of kids popped into her head. Tommy with a little boy and girl who had crystal blue eyes and medium dark hair with a slight curl in it.

She caught herself smiling at her reflection and forced herself to get back to work. She had a midday appointment to check out a new restaurant on the East Side in over an hour and had already convinced Julie to tag along with her.

It had been hard to do, but she had finally told her

neighbor what it was she did for a living. Julie had been happily surprised and excited.

When her new cell phone rang, she picked it up, happy for the detraction.

"You bitch. How dare you give my name to the police. They interviewed me and my husband like we were common criminals." Silvia Hughes' voice was calm and demanding at the same time.

"I'm sure..." She started to say, only to be interrupted.

"Stay away from us. We won't pay you or your sister a dime and as for that brat, you can keep him. He's not my husband's and you'll never get anything from us."

She heard the click and looked down at her cell phone and frowned. How had the woman gotten her new number that quickly? Then she remembered how much money the senator had and tossed her phone down in disgust.

Less than fifteen minutes later, there was a knock at her door and Julie walked in wearing one of her best outfits.

"Are you ready for our undercover mission?" she asked, looking like she would jump out of her skin.

"Undercover?" Marina had a hard time shaking herself from the bad mood.

"Sure, it's kind of like being a spy, isn't it?"

Mari had never thought of it like that before. "I suppose it is." She smiled. "Well, now I have a perfect partner." She stood up and stretched and grabbed her purse and coat.

They made their way outside and hailed a cab to take them across town.

"How long have you been doing this?" Julie asked in the cab.

"This job? I guess it's been seven years now."

"I had no clue I was friends with someone famous." She patted her leg as Marina laughed.

Lunch was very pleasant, and Marina felt that having

Julie along made the meal go more smoothly. In the cab ride home, she questioned Julie on her thoughts about the meal, staff, and the restaurant in general. Julie provided a few insights that she would have never thought about, such as how the wait staff had not only been kind but how they had all looked happy to be doing their job.

"It shows that they have a manager or boss who really cares about them. I worked at a restaurant one time where our manager treated us all like his minions. Everyone walked around trying to figure out how to piss him off all day long. It really showed to our customers and the place ended up closing down less than a year later."

They stopped by a grocery store on the way back and decided to walk home instead of taking a cab. As they walked the aisles, Julie with her cart and Marina with hers, they chatted about Trent.

"So, is he officially"—her friend air-quoted— "moving in with you?"

Marina laughed. "No, not officially. I think it's just until this whole scare blows over. Besides, my place is too small for the three of us. You should see his place." She cringed and remembered how it had looked the last time she'd seen it. "He's having it remodeled right now, and I think he just wants to make sure we're okay."

Julie sighed and leaned against the refrigerator door. "He is great with Tommy, isn't he?"

Marina nodded and watched as her friend opened the glass door. When the reflection of a large black man showed in the glass, she felt the hair on her neck stand up. She'd seen the man outside of the restaurant across town. It couldn't be the same man, could it? She turned her head slightly to get a better look at him, but he was gone. The rest of their shopping trip, her mind was preoccupied with trying to get a good glimpse of the man, who was obviously not shopping. She kept asking herself why the senator would hire another man to watch her. Then she wondered if it was Silvia who had hired this one.

The huge man had a small basket in his rather large hands, but so far, the only item he carried was a small case of AA batteries. He'd followed them down almost every aisle in the store. When both of their carts were almost full, they walked up to check out and she wondered how they were going to carry everything the few blocks back to their building.

As they checked out she noticed that the man wasn't far behind. She juggled her bags until she could carry her cell phone in her right hand. Julie talked to her like nothing was wrong, and Marina wanted it that way.

When they were less than a block from their building, her phone rang. Glancing down, she saw Trent's face on her screen and sighed with relief.

"Hello?"

"Hi, where are you?"

"Just coming up to the building now."

"From which direction?"

"We've been to the market."

"Hang tight, I'll come and help." She heard a click and less than a minute later, she watched as he jogged towards her.

When she turned to hand him some bags, she noticed the man was still following them. Gripping Trent's arm, she whispered, "I think that man in the green pants and blue jacket a few yards behind me has been following us."

She watched as Trent tensed and looked over her shoulder. Then he laughed and waved towards the man. "Yeah, he has. That's Javan."

She watched in amazement as the man walked quickly towards them. "Hey," he said in a very thick Jamaican accent. "I'm sorry if I scared you."

Marina watched as Trent shook his hand warmly. "Marina, this is Javan. He's going to be watching you, making sure nothing happens."

"Hello." She felt herself relax a little. Then her mind sharpened and she realized what Trent had just said. He'd actually hired someone to follow her and watch her. Like a babysitter. She tried not to glare at the man since she didn't want to make a scene in the middle of her block.

"Here, let me help you with those," Javan said, grabbing a few bags from Julie since Trent had already grabbed most of Marina's. Marina watched Julie blush and hand over her bags to the large man.

"This is my neighbor, Julie," she said, making the quick introductions.

"I know." He nodded and smiled at her friend.

"Of course," she said, looking over at Trent with a glare.

She watched Javan help Julie into her apartment down the hallway as Trent unlocked her door with the set of keys she'd given him.

When she walked into the kitchen, he had set the bags down and was frowning at them.

"I don't know where you expect to put all this in this small kitchen. But I'm sure you have your ways." He turned and smiled at her.

She stood just inside the doorway, her arms crossed over her chest. "I can't believe you hired someone to babysit me." She felt like tapping her toe but stopped herself from doing so.

His eyebrows shot up. "Babysit?"

"That man!" She motioned towards her closed door.

Trent laughed. "Javan is no babysitter. He's a lethal weapon in at least a dozen countries." He leaned back and crossed his arms over his chest, mimicking her stance.

Marina paled. "He's a killer?" She looked towards the doorway. "I left Julie alone…"

Trent quickly walked across the room and took her shoulders in his hands, forcing her to turn and look at him. "He's a protector. I mentioned to a good buddy of mine who runs a security service about our scare, and he sent Javan to help out for a while. No harm was done."

She sighed and closed her eyes.

"He'll be watching Tommy as well."

She looked up at Trent and sighed again. "I suppose it couldn't hurt for a while."

OVER THE NEXT FEW WEEKS, everything seemed to run smoothly. The new building had passed its final inspection and was just awaiting his occupancy certificate. He'd hired most of his new staff and was eagerly awaiting opening week, which was quickly approaching.

He was living full-time at Marina's and was thoroughly enjoying his time with her and Tommy. He had yet to talk to her about what he really did, but part of him still wondered if she had known all along. Even Manhattan Nights was getting back into the full swing of things. It had been almost six months since Marina's review had been published and now customers were crowding back into the restaurant.

His apartment was being redecorated with Marina's help. He had asked her to organize his stuff and to help with the placement of the new furniture he'd bought.

He was standing in the back room of Manhattan Nights one Sunday night when he heard a commotion up front.

When he walked out front, he found several people arguing, and he headed towards the growing crowd. It didn't take long for him to realize what the situation was; he'd seen it a million times. Someone was drunk, and everyone was trying to convince them to go home and sleep it off. It took almost ten minutes of his time to pour the older gentlemen into a cab with his kids and grandkids.

When he was done, Trent walked back into the restaurant and bumped into a familiar body. When he grabbed her shoulders, his first response was to pull her closer, but then he remembered where he was and what he was wearing.

"Marina?" He saw the surprise on her face and then watched recognition and, finally, anger cross those dark eyes of hers.

"Is it true?" He could see her shaking. Her jacket was miss-buttoned, and her hair looked like she'd run all the way here from her place.

Not wanting to cause another scene, he pulled her along until finally, he closed the door to his office behind them.

"Marina," he started, but before he could think of something to say, she walked towards him and shoved a finger into his chest.

"You're the owner of Manhattan Nights? A restaurant I reviewed in this article?" It was then that he noticed that she was carrying a clipping of the newspaper. She'd wadded it up and was waving her fist around.

"I can explain," he started, but again no words would come out of his mouth.

"You knew," she said in a low voice, and he could see that she'd pieced it all together.

"Yes."

"You've been using me."

"No." He started to walk towards her, but she jumped back.

"How did you know? Is it true?" She waved the paper in front of him and he was even more confused.

"Is what true?"

"That you hired someone to hunt me down, so you could seek your revenge on the person who caused your precious restaurant to fail?"

"No!" He walked closer to her and took the paper from her hands. Fear shot through him when he saw the deep red writing over a clipping of her article about Manhattan Nights.

He's found you. He lied to you. He's using you.

"It's not true." He looked up into her eyes, begging her to give him a chance to explain.

"Did you think I would change my mind?"

"No. I thought you were on the take," he blurted out and instantly regretted his words. "Wait." He grabbed her arm as she tried to walk past him. "That's not what I think now."

She pushed his hand off her arm and glared at him. "You used me. That day in the coffee shop. You already knew who I was?"

He nodded.

"And you continued to keep it from me this whole time?"

He nodded again and then felt something break as he watched her turn towards the door. When she reached for the handle, she turned and looked back at him. "Don't bother coming back to my place." She turned and walked out and for the first time in his life, he felt true panic setting in.

The rest of the night, he worked in a daze. Finally, one of his employees mentioned to him that he looked like shit, so he left early. Heading back to his place was one of the loneliest things he'd ever done. Just a few months ago, he was happy walking across the street alone, walking into his apartment alone. Now, however, it felt empty. He felt empty.

He stood in his doorway and looked at his place. The new furnishings were wonderful; Marina's organization skills had made everything look better and cleaner somehow.

When he walked into the kitchen, he remembered how

she'd looked in the blue dress with the skirt hiked up and her hair loose in his hands. Closing his eyes, he thought about never seeing her again and his heart broke.

Then he remembered Tommy's face when he'd seen the bald eagles at the zoo and it broke a little more. He wanted them back. No, he needed them back. But he needed a plan first. He had to prove to them that it hadn't all been a lie. His future depended on it.

When he finally got up the nerve to show up at her door, the place was empty and a "For Rent" sign hung in the window. He knocked on Julie's door, but there was no answer. There was only one thing he could think of to do to get her attention, and he knew just the man to set it all up.

CHAPTER 14

*M*arina was covered in sweat and dust. It had taken her three days to find the right place and now, as she lugged the last box up the stairs at her new place, she told herself that everything was going to be all right. Of course, she was lying to herself.

Tommy was still asking about Trent. When was he going to be coming around? Was he going to be moving in with them? Why wasn't he coming to see them? Was he mad at them?

So many questions, she still didn't know what to say to him. Should she tell him that Trent had lied to them? Broken her heart? Every evening she lay in her bed and reached over to his side. When she found it empty, she would cry herself back to sleep.

Why? Why had he done this? She'd thought he was the one, the one man she could finally feel free and safe enough with to dream about settling down. Now, she was having to rip herself and Tommy out of their little home and into another apartment just to escape the feeling that Trent would walk in the door at any moment.

So far, since that day she'd confronted him, they hadn't heard a word from him. Had they really meant that little to him that he wouldn't even try to win them back?

Julie had been shocked when she'd told her friend the situation. She'd done what all good friends would have—she bad-mouthed him until Marina had felt a little better about her decision.

Now, as she stood looking at her somewhat larger apartment, she wondered if she had made the right choice. She should have demanded an explanation. He had to have a reason for dragging their relationship out for almost three months. Right?

As she unpacked, she found herself not caring where everything went. She tossed things in drawers, hung clothes out of color order, and even ended up putting a few dishes in with the pans. This is what he'd done to her. He'd turned her into a slob. When she found the kitchen knives in one of the desk drawers, she sat down on the floor and cried.

Over the next few weeks, she went back to work. Each night she would try to organize the new apartment, and each night she would fail. Tommy took to working in his room after dinner and she allowed him the time. Eventually, he stopped asking about Trent and she was happy, or so she kept telling herself.

It wasn't long after that she received a phone call from Reggie with a personal request from the mayor himself to review a new restaurant. He didn't give her a name, just an address, and told her what time to be there tomorrow. She added it to her schedule on the following day and realized that life would go on without Trent and that she needed to focus on Tommy and herself now.

When she stopped in front of the recently remodeled building the following evening, she paused and stared up at the sign for almost five minutes. There, in thin white letters was her name. Knowing it had to be a coincidence, she shook her head clear and walked through the front doors.

The place was gorgeous. The gleaming wood tables were covered in classic cream-colored tablecloths. The high-back chairs were a warm leather, accenting the light colors and making the place feel comfortable and intimate.

There were a million tiny lights hanging from the ceiling in an intricate, chaotic design. Tall private booths lined the inside walls and surrounded a two-story spiral staircase. She'd never seen such a massive structure. A large crystal chandelier hung over the gleaming stairs and railing.

She heard someone clear their throat behind her and realized she'd been standing in the entrance, gawking at the view. Then she realized that the place was completely empty.

"I'm sorry. I hadn't realized you weren't open yet." She backed up towards the door.

"We are open. Follow me, please." She looked around again as the thin man motioned for her to follow him towards the staircase.

"How long ago did you open?" she asked, climbing the stairs. She enjoyed the rich feel of the gleaming wood in her hand as she followed him up the stairs. Her eyes caught every detail of the room as she looked at it from above.

"Grand opening is set for later this weekend."

"Oh, but I thought…" She dropped off when she saw that the upstairs, a long narrow room that normally would have housed a dozen or more tables, had one small table set for two in the middle of the floor with tall candles surrounding it. Then she noticed the man standing next to one of the chairs and her back stiffened as she stopped in the middle of the floor. The thoughts about the beauty of the room and the building were replaced by fear and anger.

The maître d' had quietly disappeared, leaving them alone in the massive room.

"Please." Trent motioned towards the chair. "Give me a chance."

Looking into his eyes, she decided she couldn't deny him this one chance to explain himself. After all, she'd assumed that he had been going along fine without her. Now, she could see that his eyes were tired and full of fear that she would walk out of the room forever.

She walked forward and sat in the chair he'd pulled out and had been holding for her without saying a word.

He walked around and sat down across from her.

"Thank you. First I'd like a chance to explain myself." When she nodded, he continued. "Since your review of Manhattan Nights, I'd been looking for M. Jensen. I'd read a few online articles claiming that the elusive M. Jensen was actually a woman instead of a man. There were even some grainy photos of you entering a half dozen places." He sighed and then continued. "I'd hired my security friend Ethan to find out who was trying to destroy my business, thinking that you were on the take or being blackmailed. Then I saw you walking towards me that day on the sidewalk outside of the coffee shop and I knew it was you. After talking to you, I knew I had to find out more."

He paused to pour them a glass of wine, which he took a sip from, then he quickly returned to his story. "Then something changed." He set his glass down and looked her in the eyes. "You confirmed my new thoughts about your character, that you hadn't been bought or threatened into tearing my restaurant down. I know I should have come clean then, but..." He shook his head and closed his eyes. "It was the hardest thing I've ever done in my life, letting you walk away that day." He opened his eyes and she could see the anguish in them. "I deserved it. I deserved to be left to suffer. I should have told you once I knew I'd fallen for you." He shook his head. "Not just you, but Tommy as well. That kid means so much to me. Please, Marina, give me another chance. I promise you I will never lie to you again." He sat across from her, his eyes pleading with hers as tears streamed down her face. She'd sat there, silently listening to his speech, knowing that he'd probably gone over it a million times.

"Trent, I don't know if—"

"Wait," he broke in. "Before you say anything, please." He clapped his hands and two men in dark suits came in carrying plates. "I've made something special, just for you." He nodded to his staff and they disappeared as quickly as they had arrived.

"Trent?" She looked down at the gorgeous food. Then she smiled and looked up at him. "Are you trying to buy me off?"

He chuckled nervously. "You'll let me know if it worked?" She nodded. "Good. I can wait for your answer until after the food."

She looked up at him and sighed, then nodded.

"How's Tommy?" he asked, as she took up her fork and knife.

She sighed again. "He misses you. He's mad at me for not letting him see you. He's taken to staying in his room most nights."

His eyebrows furrowed. "It's not your fault. If you want, I can talk to him."

She smiled and nodded.

"Does he like the new place?" Surprise must have shown on her face. "I stopped by shortly after you moved out and talked to Julie the next day. You didn't have to move, you know."

She nodded and looked down at her food, which she had yet to try. "There were too many ghosts. Besides, the place felt empty."

"I know what you mean." She glanced up at him. "I'm

hardly at my place now. Even though the place is finished, it just doesn't feel right."

She cut a piece of the dark meat and took it up to her mouth. When the richness of it hit her tongue, her eyes closed, and she stifled a low moan. A zip of flavor flooded her senses. Her mouth watered for more and she actually felt goose bumps rising on her arms. She took up another piece, thinking it must have been a fluke. The next taste was even better than the first.

"Do you like it?" he asked, his eyes on her every move.

She didn't have any words, so instead, she nodded her head and took another bite. She tried the rice and gravy and then moved on to the spray of vegetables.

"It looks like you've finally found a wonderful chef," she said in between bites.

He chuckled, causing her to pause with the next bite in midair.

"I cooked everything you see here tonight. I don't know what happened when you visited Manhattan Nights before, but this"—he nodded to the plate— "is the quality you should have gotten there."

She shook her head and frowned. "This is nothing like the meal I ate."

He nodded. "I know. I still don't know how you were served the food you got. I fired the first chef, thinking it was just his lack of experience, but then you wrote that cursed letter." He chuckled and then frowned. "Then I knew someone was sabotaging me. I've had to watch all my employees very carefully, so much so that I think that whoever it was tried a different tactic."

Realization hit her. "You think they broke into your place and trashed it?"

He nodded. "They hit this place too. I hired a security

company to watch both places. I think that's why they stole your phone and threatened me with your safety."

"Who would do something like that?" she asked, taking a sip of her wine. The smoothness of it caused some of the sicknesses about the whole situation to settle a little.

He shrugged his shoulders. "I've had Ethan and his team on it for weeks." Shaking his head, he frowned down at his forgotten plate. He was silent for a while, and she realized that she knew what she had to do. She knew that she didn't want to live another day, spend another night alone without him. Even Tommy was becoming unbearable without Trent around.

"Did you really name this place after me?" she asked.

When he nodded his head and smiled a little, she set down her fork, stood up and walked around the table until she stood before him. He quickly got up, almost knocking the table over in the process. She chuckled and took his face in her hands.

"Trent, I would love it if you would come back home with me where you belong."

He smiled and shook his head. "No. I know it's a lot to ask, but my place is a lot bigger and Tommy would have a courtyard to play in." He pulled her closer. "Move in with me?"

She smiled. "We're pretty much still packed since I could never muster up enough willpower to unpack without you."

He leaned down and placed a soft kiss on her lips. She'd missed the feel of him next to her, the taste of his mouth against hers. When he moaned, she knew then that she'd done the right thing. They belonged together.

"Marina," he said pulling back a little, "I want you so much. I've missed you." He looked into her eyes then looked around and frowned. "Come back to my place, just for a while. Then we'll go get Tommy and some of your stuff." She nodded and took his hand as he practically dragged her down the stairs.

TRENT FELT like running back to his place, but he knew that if he carted Marina over his shoulders like he wanted, they would get too many looks. Instead, he hailed a cab and waited patiently as they drove a dozen blocks back to his place. He held her hand in his and pulled her close every turn they made. By the time the cab stopped, he was kissing her until they were both breathless. He threw some money at the cabbie and they rushed up his stairs quickly. When he opened the door, they were both still breathless and his desire had grown painful.

He didn't give her time to recover. Instead, he shut the door behind them, pushed her up against it, and took her heated mouth with his. Her hands pulled his head down to hers, her lips crushed under his as his hands roamed over the silk dress she was wearing.

He'd been happily surprised to see that she'd worn tall boots with the green silk dress. She'd left her hair down and he ran his fingers through it now, noticing how soft it was. He'd missed the feeling of it and her skin next to his.

Using just a finger, he pulled the thin strap of her dress off her left shoulder.

"I must have left my jacket in the restaurant," she said, and he could hear the nerves in her voice.

"Don't worry, I know the owner," he said, watching her skin turn pink under his gaze. When he had pushed one strap off her shoulder, he reached for the other one as her fingers pulled his dinner jacket off his shoulders.

Her head fell back against the wood door when he dipped his head down and tasted the skin just below her ear. When her fingers started tugging on his buttons, he moved back and pulled the shirt from his pants.

"You are so beautiful," he said, coming back to her. The dress had a thin belt the same color. He reached down and pulled it open and, to his surprise, the dress fell open to her waist. "Nice." He smiled up at her and then used a finger to pull it open even further.

She was wearing silk underneath silk, and his mind fogged when he noticed the garter belts.

"I love these," he said running a finger over the smoothness of it and her skin just below the silk.

She smiled and wrapped her arms around his shoulders and kissed him. He hiked her legs up around his hips and took her right there against the doorway to their place. The sweet sounds she made as he claimed her were his undoing. By the time his release found him, he knew without a doubt that he didn't want to spend a day without holding her in his arms.

"It's getting late," she said against his skin. They had ended up on his new sofa, her almost-naked body sprawled on top of his. She pulled back and looked down at him. "Did you hear me?" she asked, smiling at him.

"Hmm." He nodded. "Who's watching Tommy? Julie?"

She nodded. "She and the boys came over to the new place for a while." She glanced at the large clock over his fireplace and frowned.

"Don't worry, we'll go get him." He sat up, almost dislodging her in the process. "Oops," he laughed as he picked her up and carried her to where most of her clothes were. "We can take a cab. It'll be faster."

She nodded as she wrapped the green silk around her and tied it shut with the belt.

"What do you call that kind of dress?" he asked, hardly taking his eyes from her as she slipped on her tall boots.

"It's a wrap dress." She frowned and looked at him. "Why?"

He smiled. "You'll have to buy more of those."

She laughed.

"Here." He reached into his closet and pulled out one of his jackets. "It's probably gotten a lot colder out there."

She wrapped it around the silk dress as they walked out the front door.

Less than ten minutes later, they stopped in front of a newer brick building. He'd seen the places going up a few years back and had always wondered what they looked like inside.

"How'd you find this place?" he asked as they walked up the short set of stairs near the back.

"Luck. Julie had been on a waiting list to move in for almost a year, but after hearing what I'd gone through, she gave her spot up for us. Besides, she can't afford the new place with Juan's father not paying child support anymore." She stopped and turned towards him when she reached her door. "Did you know your big friend has been seeing her?"

"Who?" He frowned.

"Javan." She smiled and unlocked her door. "It appears he's crazy about Julie and the boys. I wouldn't be surprised if..." She stopped dead when she saw a blonde woman sitting on her couch across from Julie. Tommy stood in the middle, crying. When he saw Marina and Trent standing in the doorway, he threw himself across the room and into their waiting arms.

"I don't want to go. Tell her to go away!" he kept shouting.

Marina looked at the other woman like she'd seen a ghost. When she stood up, Trent realized instantly who it was and his heart broke.

"Trina?" Marina finally stuttered out. "How?"

"You didn't make it easy for me to find you." Her sister's

voice was higher than hers. Too high, in Trent's opinion. "When you moved, you forgot to message me."

"I did. I sent a text to the last number I had for you, but it bounced."

Trina walked over and pulled Tommy from her sister's arms. "I didn't get a text," she said, looking between Marina and Trent. "Is this how you've been watching my son?" She crossed her arms over her chest and frowned at the pair.

"What?" Marina blinked a few times. "I was working tonight."

"Right. Well, I'm back now." She turned to Tommy and grabbed his arm tightly. "Let's go pack up your things; we're leaving for Boston tonight."

Marina stepped forward and put a hand on Tommy's shoulder as he cried and shook his head no.

"Listen, I really appreciate you watching him for so long. It's taken me a while to get back on my feet. Now, if you don't mind, I have a very busy schedule."

Marina's eyes heated. "Julie"—she looked at her friend—"would you take Tommy into his room and stay with him please?"

Julie nodded and gently picked up the crying boy who was still screaming that he didn't want to go.

"Trent, I'd like you to stay since this affects you as well." She took his hand and stopped him from following Julie and Tommy. He nodded and gripped her hand more firmly.

"I don't know what has gotten into you, but you are not taking that boy tonight. You can't just barge in here after a year, two months, eight days, and..." —she looked at her watch— "two hours and expect to snatch him away from us with no warning."

She dropped Trent's hand and took a step towards her sister. "I know you, Trina. Don't think that I don't see the red in your eyes, that shake in your hand." She motioned towards her sister's hands, which Trina quickly tucked into her long coat. "You've still got the price tag on the coat, which means you're probably going to return it tomorrow and spend the money snorting it." She put a hand up. "Your tactics might have worked on me a few years back, but you're not fooling anyone now. Tommy is not yours anymore. He's ours." She nodded towards Trent. "And if you want him back, you're going to have to fight us for him." She crossed her arms over her chest.

"Yeah!" the little boy said from the doorway.

"I'm sorry," Julie said, rushing into the room. "He got away from me."

Tommy's red eyes were now dry and full of anger. "You can't have me. I have a new mommy and daddy now. Tell her." He looked up at Trent with pleading eyes.

CHAPTER 15

Trent woke up to something heavy falling on his chest. When he opened his eyes, he saw Tommy's little face looking back down at him, a large smile on the kid's face.

"Did you really mean what you said?"

"What?" he asked, rubbing his hands over his face and wishing for another hour of sleep.

"That you won't let her take me away."

He looked at the kid again. His bright red hair was spiked up like he'd slept on his left side all night. His eyes were no longer red and puffy from crying. "Of course, I did, buddy."

"And you're going to be my new daddy?"

Trent smiled and nodded his head. "I'd like that."

"Me too," he said, placing his little hands on Trent's face, melting his heart a little more.

"Mari's making me a special breakfast. I bet she's making you some too," he said, leaning closer. "If you want, you can carry me downstairs."

Trent laughed and hoisted the kid upside down and walked down the stairs to see Marina standing in his kitchen, his "Kiss the cook" grilling apron wrapped around her shirt and jeans.

"There she is, Miss America," he sang as he walked over to her and placed a kiss on her lips while still dangling the giggling kid from his arms.

Less than four hours later, Marina and Trent sat in his lawyer's office filling out the official paperwork that would give her full custody of Tommy until a hearing could be held. Marina had Trina's original note proving that her sister had abandoned Tommy into her care over a year ago.

That, along with the criminal record the lawyer had pulled up on her sister, was enough evidence to ensure their success, at least in his lawyer's eyes. Besides, Trina still had two warrants for her arrest and the lawyer advised them to call the police next time she caused them any problems.

Tommy sat quietly in the corner, playing with his trucks while they had talked. Trent knew the kid was listening in most of the time since he never once looked like he was bored of playing with the same truck for the entire meeting.

As they all walked away from the building holding hands, Tommy in the middle, Trent felt like everything was finally coming together. He loved the kid and would do anything he could to make sure he stayed with Marina and him.

Hell, he could even imagine adding a kid of their own to the mix, maybe even two.

"How about stopping off and picking up a few more items from our place. The movers won't be there until tomorrow and I could use a few more things."

"Sure, why not?" He smiled down at the boy, who looked a little unsure.

When they arrived there, the door to Marina's place was cracked open. Trent pushed Tommy into Marina's hands and told her to go next door to call the police. Instead of waiting there for them this time, he crept inside and listened. He could hear someone moving around in the back and picked up a bat that was leaning against the wall in the entryway. He was glad he had left it for her at her old place and that she had brought it along to the new place. When he rushed into Tommy's room, he found Trina tossing the boy's things around the room.

"What are you doing here?" he demanded loudly, scaring her so that she dropped his school backpack.

"Oh, it's you." She turned and picked up the backpack like it was no big deal to be breaking into her sister's place. "I left something with Tommy and I need it back." She glanced up at him and gave him a look like he was bothering her.

"You have no right to go through Tommy's things," he said.

"What's going on?" Marina said from the doorway. "Trina, what on earth?" She rushed into the room and snatched Tommy's bag from her sister.

"It's no big deal. I gave something to Tommy to watch for me, now I need it back." She shrugged her shoulders and crossed her arms over her chest.

"Is that why you came back?" Marina asked. She bit her bottom lip then said, "Brandon said you had something of his. Did you leave it with Tommy?"

"It's none of your business. Now, if you'll just let me look for it…" She got down on her hands and knees and started going through the contents of Tommy's bag, which she'd poured out.

"Here," Tommy said from the doorway. "You can have it." He held out the red truck towards her. "If you'll leave me alone and never come back." He tossed the red truck towards Trina. "Go away!" he shouted when she jumped towards the truck.

Just then, two officers with their guns drawn came

rushing into Tommy's room, causing the little boy to rush towards Trent in fear.

"Woah!" Trent said, raising his hands. "It's all right."

Marina stepped closer and started to explain while Trina pulled out a small USB drive from the cab of the truck and tucked it into her jeans. Then she tossed the truck on the ground and looked for a way to escape.

"Did you authorize your sister to come into your apartment?" one of the officers asked.

"Yes," Trina piped in. "Mari said I could come back and get a few things. Didn't you, sister?" Trina walked over and took her sister's arm playfully.

Marina wasn't going along with it. "No." She shook her head. "She broke in and started going through Tommy's things."

"Tommy's my son!" Trina shouted. "I have the right—"

"No, you don't." Marina turned on her sister.

"Officers, if I may?" Trent set Tommy back down on the floor and walked over to Trina. "I believe this"—he reached in and took out the drive— "might be of importance." Trina tried to grab the drive from his hand, but he yanked it away and handed it to the officer.

"Give me that. It's mine," Trina yelled, now trying to grab the drive from the officer. His partner quickly rolled her around and held her at bay.

"Calm down, miss." He tried to hold her steady, but now Trina was kicking at the other officer and clawing the one holding her back while screaming that it was hers.

Marina rushed over and shielded Tommy from witnessing the scene. Trent stood back and thought about helping, but the two officers quickly had her cuffed and subdued.

Finally, they sat her down on Tommy's bed and started asking her questions.

"What's on the drive?" the younger officer asked.

"It's mine," Trina said, big tears coming into her eyes.

"Ma'am, we can easily find out what's on this." He held it up.

Trina's tears had started to turn worse. "He promised me money. Enough money that I wouldn't have to worry anymore," she cried.

"Who?"

"Brandon?" Marina asked, stepping forward.

Trina nodded her head. "He wants the drive back. At first, I held onto it to make sure he didn't take Tommy, but then…" She looked at the little boy in Trent's arms. "I guess I just got used to not having him around." She shrugged her shoulders. "Life was easier without him always asking questions." She looked away from the kid and Trent walked out of the room with Tommy in his arms.

He took him down the stairs and sat down on the steps outside the building.

"I'm sorry about what your mom said." Trent rested his elbows on his knees and watched the traffic go by.

"I don't care," Tommy said, tears sliding down his chubby cheeks. "She wasn't a good mom, anyway." He wiped a tear with the back of his hand and looked down at his shoes.

"Still, she's your mom."

He shrugged his shoulders. "You're better at being a parent." He looked up at him. "You still want me, right?"

Trent smiled as he felt his heart skip. "Yeah, Marina and I would give up everything for you."

"Cool. I guess that's all that matters." Tommy looked back down at his hands. "Would it be okay if I called you Dad? I've never had one before. Not one that I've known."

"I'd like that." Trent picked the kid up and hugged him just as Marina came out and sat next to them.

"You okay?" she asked Tommy, running her fingers over his face.

"Yeah. Trent said I can call him Dad now." He smiled, and she smiled back.

They stood back and watched her sister being taken away in a police car. When they went back inside, Tommy went to go pack up a few toys and clothes to take to their new place.

"How's it going?" Trent nodded towards the door.

"They took her in for the outstanding warrants."

"I figured as much."

"But Trent, she has proof that the senator drugged and raped her. I guess it was on the USB drive."

"I thought they had an affair."

"So, did everyone else. But if what she told us is true, that USB drive has the evidence to not only ruin Brandon Hughes but to lock him away for years."

Trent shook his head and whistled. "Crazy."

"I know. She hid it in Tommy's truck and just gave it to a seven-year-old to hold. Why didn't she give it to me when the senator was threatening to take Tommy away a year ago?"

He shook his head. "Maybe she thought she could sell it?"

"I guess. I don't know if I can trust anything she says anymore." Marina frowned and shook her head. "I had hoped that she was getting clean all this time." She took a step towards him and wrapped her arms around him. "I feel so bad that I didn't do more for her."

He shook his head and put his finger under her chin until she looked at him. "You did what you had to do to keep that little boy safe. You're a wonderful aunt and are going to be the best mother ever."

She smiled and kissed him.

THE NEXT DAY was a busy one. They had less than three days before Marina's officially opened. His new staff was running around making sure everything was in order. There were trial runs during lunch and dinner with the staff's families and friends filling the dining rooms, trying every dish on the menu.

Nothing left the kitchen that he or one of his trusted staff didn't inspect. Everything was running smoothly. By the day before the grand opening, he was sure that it would be a huge success.

Several of his friends from college had made reservations for opening night, and he was excited to see them. Mitch and Carter had been there for him all throughout school and had helped him open Manhattan Nights. Now both of them were happily married. They had both chosen to move out of New York and start families up on the coast of Maine.

Even his mother was making an appearance. She usually tried avoiding the big city in the fall, but she was flying in early tomorrow morning and staying at her usual suite at the Ritz. He was excited and nervous to have his mother meet the woman he wanted to spend the rest of his life with. He knew that they would get along wonderfully, but that didn't stop him from worrying.

Marina and he had been trying to avoid watching television the last few days since her sister was all over the news. Apparently, the USB drive held a little more than she'd led them to believe. There was no proof of rape, but plenty of drugs and dirty sex involved.

Trina was still locked away for the warrants, but Marina had hired a lawyer to help make sure that she wouldn't spend the rest of her life behind bars. He understood why she needed to help her sister out. After all, she'd signed the legal paperwork giving up her rights to Tommy the day after they had arrested her.

Now all he had to do was get through tomorrow evening and then everything would fall into place. He stopped outside his new office door and looked down at the small box that had just been delivered and smiled. Walking in, he opened his desk safe and placed the engagement ring in it and leaned back to dream about his future life with Marina and Tommy.

When his phone rang, he smiled and answered, "I was just thinking about you."

"Trent?" Marina's voice was low and muffled. "Someone's following me."

"Where are you?" He stood up ready to sprint into action.

"I'm about two blocks from the house. It's too dark to see..." she said, and he could hear that she was getting breathless.

"Can you get inside a public place?" he asked, sprinting towards the door.

"No." He heard some rustling, and then her line went dead.

As he ran to grab a cab, he dialed her phone again. When she didn't answer on the third ring, he dialed 911.

He arrived at his place just as the first police car drove up. His eyes had been scanning the dark sidewalk for Marina the entire ride over. Using his key, he rushed inside, knowing already that she wasn't there.

He'd tried calling her cell a dozen times on the short ride over; still, there was no answer.

He filled the officers in on what had happened, and they decided to drive the streets to see if they could find her. Trent called Julie to see if maybe Marina had shown up there.

Julie wanted to rush over and help look, but he asked her to stay with Tommy instead since he was spending the night with her.

"Julie don't tell him anything is wrong."

"I won't. I just put on a movie. Keep me posted."

"Thanks, I will," Trent said, a little breathless from rushing down the street, searching.

If only she'd given him cross streets, he thought as he jogged down the streets looking for her. He was circling his block when something caught his eye. Rushing over, he bent down and picked up Marina's new cell phone. The screen was cracked and there was a spot of blood on the corner.

CHAPTER 16

Marina woke with something sticky running down her eyes. There was a cloth that smelled of burnt toast shoved in her mouth, gagging her. She had a hard time adjusting her eyes and when she moved her head, everything felt like it was spinning.

It was too dark to see where she was, but judging by the cool, moist atmosphere, she was betting she was underground somewhere.

She tried to move her hands and feet, but they were tied too tightly. Just then, there was a noise and her head snapped up, searching for what had made the sound.

"You just wouldn't stay away from him," a deep voice said from the dark corner.

She moaned and blinked a few times, trying to get her eyes to adjust.

"He has to learn. I told him to stay away from you." The voice was growing louder and getting closer to her.

Marina tried to ball herself up and get farther away. She couldn't tell if it was a male or female voice, but she had started to see an outline in the darkness.

"You'll just sit right here, nice and quiet, and burn!" When the woman screamed, the voice triggered something, and Marina had a flashback. The memory came to her quickly.

It was her first visit to Manhattan Nights. She'd been seated, and a male waiter had taken her order, but when her food arrived, it was delivered by a tall, chubby, blonde woman. She'd smiled down at Marina like she'd had a secret. It had kind of creeped her out, but she'd turned her focus on the food instead.

Then she remembered that the same lady had delivered her meal on her second pass at Manhattan Nights. She didn't know who the woman was or why she was trying to destroy Trent, but she desperately knew she needed to get out of there.

She started moaning and trying to talk, hoping the woman would remove her gag.

"Shut up! You don't get to talk," the woman said, taking a step closer so that Marina's eyes finally focused on the woman's face. It was the same woman, but this time, instead of a white uniform, she was wearing all black. Her arms and face were covered in soot and dirt.

Looking down, she realized her dress slacks and coat were covered in the same grime.

"I'm tired of always being second." The woman started walking around the small room. "Second in command in the kitchen, second choice in his bed." She turned and glared down at her and then pointed a finger right at her face. "He wouldn't have known you existed if I hadn't tried to punish him for passing me up for a head chef. I deserved that position! Of course, I knew who the great M. Jenkins was." She giggled. "New York's biggest secret, but I'm not stupid. I saw the pictures of you online, read all about who you were. It was easy for me to watch out for you when you came into the restaurant." She stepped back and took a deep breath and shook her head. "When I tried to get closer to Trent, all of a sudden he didn't have time for me. Because of you!" She screamed and shook her head again, then used her hands to smooth down her shirt, smearing more grime on them unknowingly.

"Well, he won't ignore me now." She turned and picked up a can of gasoline and proceeded to dump the fuel all around the chair Marina was tied to as Marina renewed her attempt to wiggle free and scream.

TRENT WAS STANDING in Manhattan Nights ten minutes later, talking to the police and most of his staff about conducting a door-to-door search in the neighborhood.

They had roped off the alleyway where they had found Marina's cell phone and searched everywhere for more clues as to what had happened. So far, they hadn't found anything else.

Now as he looked around at his staff, he took stock of the faces and frowned. "Where's Angie? I left her in charge tonight, so I could take Trey to the new place and have him help me out there."

"She took a break a while ago and never returned," someone piped in.

Trent's mind sharpened and he tried to remember a few details. When everyone left to start their search for Marina, he turned and rushed into the small office off the kitchen instead. He sat at the desk and pulled up the schedule for a few months ago on the computer.

Every day that Marina had visited, Angie had been on the schedule. Then he looked at the evening his place had been broken into and saw that she'd clocked out two hours before he'd arrived home. She would have had plenty of time to trash his place. He pulled open the top drawer and realized that the extra set of keys to his place, which he normally kept in the back of the drawer, were gone.

He had a sinking feeling he'd just discovered who had Marina, and he felt sick knowing that it was his fault.

He punched a few more keys on his computer to find out Angie's address. Seeing that it was only a few blocks away, he printed his screen and rushed out to give an update to the police. When he started to head out the door, he almost bumped into Angie in the hallway.

"Angie?" he gasped but then recovered quickly. "I didn't know you were still around." He noticed that her clothes were stained, and his eyes took in every detail. Her eyes were red, and he could see small veins in her forehead. Her hands were shaking like she was coming down off drugs.

"Angie, where's Marina?"

Angie's eyes zeroed in on his. "Why? Why couldn't you just stay away from her? Why couldn't you just notice me?" she screamed and took a step towards him.

He grabbed her arm and held it tight. "Where is Marina?" He shook her.

"She's nothing. The bitch will burn," she said and for the first time, he realized that she smelled of gasoline and sheer panic flooded him. His fingers tightened on her arm as he dug in.

"Where?"

She laughed, almost looking like she enjoyed the pain he was causing her. "You notice me now, don't you?"

He tried a different tactic. "Yes, I've always noticed you. You've been here since I opened this place." He dropped his hand and took a step back. If he didn't, he feared he wouldn't be able to control himself much longer.

"That's right. I've been here since the beginning and now..." She pulled out a lighter and smiled at him. He took a step towards her, but she shook her head "…I'll watch it all end." She flipped the lighter and he watched in horror as her sleeve caught first, followed quickly by her arm and torso. She didn't scream until he yanked the fire extinguisher from the wall and quickly doused the fire. Then she screamed, "No!" over and over again. He could smell her burnt clothes and flesh as the fire alarms screeched in the hallway.

"It has to burn!" Angie screamed as he tried to get her to hold still. Everywhere that he touched her, her clothes were charred. The fire hadn't burned that long, but it had gone long enough to cause some major damage to her hands and arms. She fell back against the wall and huddled up in a ball, gripping them in front of her.

Just then, his cell phone rang, and he yanked it out of his back pocket.

"Mr. Walker, this is the 911 dispatcher. We show that a fire alarm was triggered at your place on…"

"Yes, the fire is out, but we need an ambulance and the police here quickly," he broke in.

"I'll dispatch them right away. Is there anything I can do to help?"

"No, just get someone here now." He hung up and looked down at Angie. "Where is Marina?"

Angie was crying hysterically now. Her dark eye makeup had melted around her eyes, causing her to look pale and ghostlike.

"She'll still burn. Just wait and see." She started laughing. When the police arrived less than five minutes later, she was still laughing.

As the ambulance workers were wheeling her out under guard from a female officer, he stood in the charred hallway and tried to think of where Angie would have taken Marina.

"Mr. Walker?"

"Yes?" He turned to a young officer who was standing near him.

"We'll send someone over to her place and search it but, chances are, Miss Jenkins won't be there."

"I know."

"Is there somewhere you can think that Miss Boyer would have taken her?"

"No." He started pacing and walked back into his office as he rubbed his hands over his face. When he turned back towards the young officer, the man was looking at him funny.

"Sir, what's that all over your face?" He pointed towards Trent.

"What?" Trent walked over to the small mirror hanging by the door. There was dark grease all over his face. When he looked down at his hands, he realized that they were covered in the thick stuff. "I must have gotten it on me when I grabbed Angie," he said. Then he gasped. "I know where Marina is. Follow me." He rushed out of the room and ran towards the back stairway. He prayed that he was right.

MARINA CLOSED her eyes and hoped that she would be allowed to see Tommy and Trent one last time. The woman had left some time ago with a promise that it would all be over soon. She had trailed the gasoline behind her when she'd left and Marina sat there waiting for the glow under the doorway. But so far, it was still pitch dark.

Then she saw it. A thin beam of light under the doorway and her mind screamed, *No!*

Images of Tommy and Trent popped into her head. She had so much more she wanted to do with them. So much more she wanted to say to them.

She waited for the heat, for the sounds that would come with the fire. She knew there was enough gas around and on her that it would most likely be a fast whoosh. But nothing happened. Instead, she started to hear other noises, people talking, moving things around. Could that woman have come back? She held her breath and listened, and then she heard the sweetest voice ever.

"She has to be here somewhere," Trent said from behind the door.

She started screaming again. This time, maybe, he would hear her. She moved her shoulders and legs, making the chair wiggle on the cold cement floor.

"Here," someone else said. "I heard something."

Marina banged the chair again and started crying when the door flew open under the weight of Trent's shoulders. Seeing him stand in the doorway was one of the best sights she had ever seen.

He rushed towards her, pulled the rag from her mouth, and kissed her quickly.

"I thought I'd lost you," he said, pulling out a pocketknife from his jacket. He cut the rags that held her to the chair as a young cop walked over and helped remove the ones on her legs.

When she was freed, she jumped into his arms and held on as tight as she could.

A week later, Marina, Tommy, and Trent sat at the new restaurant, Marina's, surrounded by some of Trent's close family and friends to celebrate their engagement.

He looked over and smiled when he saw a tear escape his mother's eyes. She had fallen in love with Tommy and there wasn't a time in the last week that he hadn't seen the two of them together.

His mother had given up her suite at the Ritz and moved into his guest room after she'd heard what had happened to Marina.

"That poor girl. She'll need someone close while you focus on your big opening."

For his part, he'd taken as much time away from the opening as he could. He was confident that he'd hired the best staff and knew they were very capable of handling most of it themselves.

He wanted to be close to Marina as much as he could.

When he'd proposed at the hospital, after hearing that

she'd been given a clean bill of health, she'd quickly said "yes" and cried tears of joy.

Tommy had arrived shortly after and was instantly worried upon seeing their tears.

"No, honey, we're happy." Marina had pulled him into her lap on the bed. "We're going to finally be a family. See." She held up her hand and showed Tommy the ring Trent had placed on her finger. Tommy had jumped up and down and hugged them both.

Even his friends had stopped by his place after they'd heard what had happened. Eve and Carter had brought Hope, their three-week-old daughter, who had thick dark hair like her mother. Mitch and Sandi had their one-year-old boy, Johnny, who was a spitting image of his mother with his dark skin, hair, and eyes.

His friends stayed around until just before nightfall. He could tell that having the kids around helped keep Marina's mind off of the horrors she had been through earlier that day.

Tommy seemed to love holding the little baby and took his job of making sure her pacifier didn't fall out of her little mouth very seriously. After everyone had left, Tommy climbed into Marina's lap and, in a tired voice, asked if he could have a little sister soon. Trent had smiled at Marina and told the sleepy boy that he'd get right on it.

A glass chimed, bringing his attention back to the engagement party.

"I'd like to propose a toast." Mitch stood up and held up his glass. Tommy was sitting in Trent's lap, almost asleep. His little head had drooped several times in the last few minutes. Now, however, he sat up and looked across the room with big eyes.

Marina looked around the room full of people she hardly knew and some she knew very well. Julie and the boys were there, along with Javan, who apparently had become very close to the family. Marina smiled when she saw how cute everyone looked together. The boys had taken to Javan quickly and she hoped that her friend had finally found the man of her dreams.

"To Trent and Marina starting their new life," Mitch said, smiling at them.

"What about me?" Tommy asked, earning him a few laughs.

"Yes, can't forget you. To Trent, Marina, and Tommy starting their new life."

"Here, here." Everyone cheered and then drank.

This is a work of fiction. Names, characters, places, and incidents either are the product of the author's imagination or are used fictitiously, and any resemblance to actual persons, living or dead, business establishments, events or locales is entirely coincidental.

SECRET SAUCE

DIGITAL ISBN: 978-1-942896-42-5

PRINT ISBN: 978-1-942896-43-2

Copyeditor: Erica Ellis – inkdeepediting.com

Wild Bride

Corey's Catch

Tessa's Turn

The Grayton Series

Last Resort

Someday Beach

Rip Current

In Too Deep

Swept Away

High Tide

Lucky Series

Unlucky In Love

Sweet Resolve

Best of Luck

A Little Luck

Silver Cove Series

Silver Lining

French Kiss

Happy Accident

Hidden Charm

A Silver Cove Christmas

Entangled Series – Paranormal Romance

The Awakening

The Beckoning

The Ascension

Haven, Montana Series

Closer to You

Never Let Go

Holding On

Pride Oregon Series

A Dash of Love

My Kind of Love

Season of Love

Tis the Season

Dare to Love

Where I Belong

Wildflowers Series

Summer Nights

Summer Heat

Stand Alone Books

Twisted Rock

For a complete list of books:

http://JillSanders.com

ABOUT THE AUTHOR

Jill Sanders is a New York Times, USA Today, and international best-selling author of Sweet Contemporary Romance, Romantic Suspense, Western Romance, and Paranormal Romance novels. With over 55 books in eleven series, translations into several different languages, and audiobooks there's plenty to choose from. Look for Jill's bestselling stories wherever romance books are sold or visit her at jillsanders.com

Jill comes from a large family with six siblings, including an identical twin. She was raised in the Pacific Northwest and later relocated to Colorado for college and a successful IT career before discovering her talent for writing sweet and sexy page-turners. After Colorado, she decided to move south, living in Texas and now making her home along the Emerald Coast of Florida. You will find that the settings of several of her series are inspired by her time spent living in these areas. She has two sons and off-set the testosterone in her house by adopting three furry little ladies that provide her company while she's locked in her writing cave. She enjoys heading to the beach, hiking, swimming, wine-tasting, and pickleball with her husband, and of course writing. If you have read any of her books, you may also notice that there is a love of food, espe-

cially sweets! She has been blamed for a few added pounds by her assistant, editor, and fans... donuts or pie anyone?

f facebook.com/JillSandersBooks

🐦 twitter.com/JillMSanders

BB bookbub.com/authors/jill-sanders